State of Pursuit

Collapse Series #4

Summer Lane

For Grandma & Grandpa.
You're the best. I love you!

Praise for *The Collapse Series*

"The 20 year old Reedley resident is a prolific writer."

- Rick Bentley, *Fresno Bee, AP*

"State of Emergency is an engaging read that is compelling and believable."

- Roy Huff, author of the bestselling *Everville Series*

[Summer Lane] is quite a talented writer with an amazing gift for narration."

- Janice White, Editor and co-author of *Clarity: A Text on Writing*

"Cassidy Hart is a smart, snarky, scared and sassy protagonist."

- Brian Palmer, co-author of *XII: Genesis*

"At 20, Lane is establishing herself in the competitive 'Young Adult' area of writing."

- *The Reedley Exponent*

"Summer's ability to craft a compelling story seems effortless."

- Jenny Graber-Peters, Editor of *Traffic Magazine*

"Absolutely heart-stopping! Cassidy and Chris have come a long way since they first fled into the mountains...If you enjoy dystopia even a little bit, you will love this series."

- Leti Del Mar, author of *Land of the Unaltered*

"What is extraordinary is that Summer has made it so that you've come to care about these secondary characters almost as much as the main characters – Cassidy and Chris."

- Ruth Silver, author of *Orenda* and *Dead Girl Walking*

"Intense, fast-paced, never a dull moment. You feel as if you're with Cassidy every step of the way, cheering her on."

- Ellen Mansoor Collier, author of *The Jazz Age Mystery Series*

"I was totally engrossed from the first sentence until the very last period...This series is one of my favorites."

-   Michelle Kullman, *Mom with a Kindle*

Prologue

Omega POW Facility – Somewhere in L.A.

He couldn't remember the last time he'd had water. It'd been a while. He knew that much. Somewhere in the back of his mind, he realized that it had been too long. He could tell by the way he swallowed. There was no moisture left in his mouth.

There was blood on the floor.

Why? He couldn't remember that, either.

He only knew that he *was,* and for the moment, that would have to do. Survival depended on focusing his thoughts on a single point. One thought. One object. One name.

Cassidy.

"You know...it wouldn't take much to help yourself," a tall, lithe man in the corner drawled. Harry Lydell. He was handsome, impeccably dressed in an Omega uniform. Black jacket and pants, boots. Piercing blue eyes. He looked bored, watching the prisoner lean against the wall in the corner of the cell.

He was a sight. All blood and bruises. Radiating pain.

Just the way Harry liked it.

"You're stubborn," Harry continued, crossing his arms. "You remind me of someone I know. Someone *you* know." He paused, a cruel smile creeping across his lips. "Cassidy Hart."

The prisoner looked up, dirty blonde hair plastered against his unshaven face. Sweat dripped off his forehead. He said nothing. Only glared.

"Nothing has changed," Harry went on. "This is still a war. We are still enemies, and at the moment, *you* are at a disadvantage." He stopped. Waiting. "You can either divulge your secrets...or die. Because that is what *will* happen. You, Chris Young, the Commander of the beloved militias – dead. It's not quite the glorious death of a warrior you envisioned for yourself, is it? Crammed in a hole, bleeding to death?"

Chris still said nothing, but his silence spoke volumes.

Harry remained silent for a moment. Pensive. He better than anyone knew exactly what Chris Young was capable of, and what he would do to protect the people he loved the most. And right now, those people were out of Harry's reach. And that put *him* at a disadvantage. Chris Young would not give him any information regarding the militias if his life depended on it.

The fool, thought Harry. *He would give his life for anyone except himself.*

"We will talk in the morning," Harry said at last. He tilted his head, straining to get a better glimpse of Chris's face. "Don't go anywhere."

He smirked at his own joke and retreated from the cell. The door clanged shut behind him as the guards locked it tight again. The concrete hall glowed softly with generator-powered lights.

That didn't work, Harry mused internally. *If only I had something that was important to him...some**one** important...*

But there was only so much time Omega would spend interrogating Commander Young before they would simply kill him. Chris Young, like the rest of the POWs in this prison, were valuable only if they were willing to talk.

And Chris would not talk.

Chris would die first.

So die he must, in Harry's mind. That was the only logical option left.

He checked his watch, exiting the hallway. The heavy door slammed shut behind him. He entered a wide office room, desks and cubicle dividers creating a maze-like illusion. Omega officers nodded their heads in respect as they passed.

Ah. That was what he liked. Respect.

His office was here, at the opposite end of the building. A private room with a window overlooking the street below. It was a clean room, a tight one. Efficient and practical. That's how Harry preferred it.

He stood at the window with his hands clasped behind his back.

And he thought.

Of all the militia officers that Omega had managed to take prisoner, Chris Young was the most annoying – the most trouble. The man had remarkable leadership capabilities. He had, after all, taken mere civilians and turned them into a viable fighting force. One that sent Omega reeling on more than one occasion. Thanks to him – and Cassidy Hart – militias were coming out of the woodwork across the state. The country, even.

Chris Young was a threat that should be eliminated.

But Harry wasn't an impatient man.

She'll come, he thought. *And when she does, I'll kill her, too. All of them.*

Because for Harry Lydell, very few things mattered besides power, hatred and revenge. And revenge was exactly what he had in store for Chris Young and Cassidy Hart.

He would make sure of that.

Chapter One

National Guard Headquarters – Militia Forces –
The Grapevine

Rain is pouring from the heavens, freezing.

My curly red hair is soaked, sticking to my face. I pull my jacket tightly around myself, gazing across the expanse of asphalt and abandoned buildings. There are soldiers everywhere, looking like ants in the distance. They are bloody, torn, bruised and exhausted. I kneel on the roofing, perched like a bird. Watching. Waiting.

I've been up here a couple of times in the past ten hours.

Maybe, if things had been different, I could have gone back. Maybe I could have saved him. Maybe I could have saved *both* of them. I squeeze my eyes shut, tears rolling down my cheeks, hot and salty. I could have saved at least *one* of them, couldn't I?

You know that would have been impossible, my inner voice reasons. *You were outnumbered a hundred to one. Jeff's death wasn't your fault. Chris staying behind to help Max isn't your fault either.*

I feel like it's my fault. Why should I be the one to make it back alive and safe?

What if Chris is dead? It's been twenty-four hours since Manny rescued me in his biplane and brought me back to Headquarters, where our National Guard forces have amassed. Twenty-four hours since I watched Jeff Young die,

Chris's younger brother. Twenty-four hours since Derek and Max went missing and Chris promised me he'd be right behind me.

He broke that promise.

I've been scanning the horizon every hour since I got back. I've hardly slept. I've barely eaten.

And here I am. Battered, but cleared for duty.

No sign of Chris.

God, please don't let him be dead. Please. I'm begging you.

A commotion on the south side of the parking lot draws my attention. I lean forward. Someone is arriving. Soldiers straggling in on foot. My heart leaps in my chest. Chris? I jump over the ledge and swing my legs onto the rusty fire escape on the side of the building. I climb down the ladder, hit the asphalt and run across the parking lot. I bypass idling Humvees unloading injured soldiers to be carted into the medical building.

A mountain rises up at the end of the parking lot, one of the Tehachapi hills, the beginning of the Grapevine next to the I-5 Interstate running into Los Angeles. National Guardsmen are gathered around the arriving group of soldiers.

I push through the crowd. Several of the guards step aside. I am a Lieutenant here, and I am well known. When I reach the front of the crowd, I beam. Derek, lithe and blonde, is supporting Sophia Rodriguez. They're both caked in mud, filthy, bloody. But alive.

And then I frown because Chris is not with them.

The medical team hurries to the scene, helping Sophia and Derek toward the *Jack in the Box*. I have no time to say hello or exchange greetings. I lock eyes with Derek. He nods briefly, a sorrowful glance.

He knows.

I stand on the edge of the parking lot, staring into the hills. The pillars of black smoke that were poisoning the air only yesterday have already diminished. The rain has been too heavy for the fires to continue burning.

But we have pushed Omega back.

For now.

The sky is dark. Mud and rocks slide down the sides of some of the hills, piling across the freeway like manmade blockades.

Still no sign of Chris.

I turn on my heel and head back toward a restaurant set away from the freeway – the *Taco House* was its former name. Right now we're just calling it Headquarters. I enter the front door.

The National Guard's Colonel Rivera is inside, along with his officers. Many of our own militiamen are here, too. Candles inside of lamps illuminate the building. Rain pelts the windows. Rivera, a burly man with powerful, defined features barely glances at me as I step into the room. Angela Wright, a fellow militia commander, straightens up, alert. Her white hair is pulled in a tight bun. Her daughter, Vera, is standing nearby, her platinum blonde locks in a ponytail. We make brief eye contact before she looks away, staring at the maps on the counter.

"Have you sent out another search party?" I ask.

"It's on its way back," Angela replies, casting a sideways glance at Rivera. One that he doesn't return. "We'll know for certain when they get here."

I swallow a massive lump in my throat.

It's taking everything in me to hold myself together.

Everything.

I assess the crowd gathered here.

Derek, Sophia and Vera are accounted for. Angela survived. Rivera is alive. Max and Uriah haven't returned yet. Jeff is dead.

I'm alive. Barely.

I stare at the smoking cigar Colonel Rivera is nervously chewing on.

"How many of our men defected?" I say.

The word *defected* makes everyone flinch. Maybe a better word would be *betrayal*. Because that's what happened. Our own men turned against us during the battle last night. Turncoats. Spies.

Murderers.

"We don't have an exact number yet," Colonel Rivera states, briefly looking at me. "It's not as bleak as you think."

"Yes, it *is*," I snap, startled at the venom in my voice. "How did this *happen*? How did *that* many of our own men turn on us? How long have they been infiltrating our ranks?"

"A long time," Angela replies, unconsciously tensing. "A very long time."

"Not that long," Rivera says.

I glare, animosity simmering in my blood. My affection for Colonel Rivera is at zero. This man once denied the militia backup while we were under heavy fire. It's safe to say that I'm not his number one fan.

And neither was Chris.

But Chris sucked it up, took charge and worked with him anyway, my conscious says. *You should do the same, or you're going to explode. You've got to maintain control, Cassidy.*

Right. Control. Me.

I can do this.

"Can I contact the search team via radio?" I ask, moving toward the table.

"We're radio silent," Colonel Rivera growls, snapping his gaze up. "No contact."

"But I need to-"

"-We all need to know." Angela places a hand on my forearm. A dangerous move, considering the mood I'm in. "But we need to wait. They'll be here."

I slowly withdraw my arm and close my fists around the corner of the counter.

Waiting is driving me insane. I can't wait.

I won't.

"Good news, folks." Manny bursts through the front door. His gray hair is hanging in wet strands to his neck, flight goggles and cap tight against his forehead. His coat is dripping, his face is covered in ash and soot. "They're back," he says. And this time, he looks right at me.

"They saw them."

Last year, an EMP destroyed the technological infrastructure of the United States of America. Technology – everything from vehicles to microwave ovens – died in an instant. Long story short, it screwed everything up.

Everything.

The country collapsed, anarchy ensued, people panicked and Omega – a shadow army arisen from the chaos – rolled in and invaded. I was living in Culver City, California at the time of the EMP – also known as an electromagnetic pulse. I barely escaped with my life from Los Angeles. I got separated from my father, and in the process teamed up with a former Navy SEAL named Chris Young. In the last year I've been imprisoned in an Omega slave labor camp, joined a militia called the *Freedom Fighters*, found my father, teamed up with the National Guard to fight Omega and barely survived a devastating betrayal by our own militiamen.

On the bright side, the militia forces and the remnants of the National Guard combined have pushed Omega back towards Los Angeles. On the negative side, we've lost a lot of good men and women – including our militia commander and the love of my life, Chris Young.

Not everything is rosy.

We're stuck in a constant state of war. Despite our best efforts to fight against the threat of Omega – and drive back a five million-man army coming from China – we still have a long way to go. Our communication with the rest of the country is limited, and besides rumors, what's going down on the east coast is anyone's guess. Nothing is completely clear, and that adds to our frustration. The enemy we fight is mostly a mystery. Where did they come from? How did they invade so quickly?

We may never have all the answers.

As for me, I watched one of my dearest friends die last night.

Jeff Young, Chris's younger brother, was shot in the neck. Derek and Sophia survived, but there's still no sign of Max or Uriah. Alexander Ramos – a gruff Lieutenant and a friend of Chris's – went MIA before the battle even really began.

So many people have died.

So many bad things have happened.

But we continue to fight, to survive, because none of us are willing to give into Omega. They've killed so many innocent people. Wiped out the cities with chemical weapons, nuked the urban epicenters on the east coast, slaughtered the innocent civilians on the west coast in concentration and slave labor camps. They have had no mercy on us, so we cannot afford to have any on them.

It's fight or die these days.

My father, the Commander of the *Mountain Rangers* in the Sierra Nevada Mountains, remains with his men to defend the rural and mountain population. Those of us who chose to combine our forces with the National Guard to fight Omega were stationed for some time in Fresno, California, before deploying to the Chokepoint – where we are right now, at the base of the Tehachapi Mountains in southern California.

I am a Lieutenant in the militia, in charge of a platoon of snipers. My Commander is Chris, and my fellow officers are my friends. We are here purely on a volunteer basis, and although Colonel Rivera can give us orders, our loyalty ultimately lies with Chris.

Chris, who may be dead, and without whom I would not be alive.

The man that I will find, whatever the cost.

Chapter Two

"What did they see?" I ask.

I am the first one to reach Manny. I clutch his forearm, desperate for good news. He gently squeezes my shoulder, a moment of kindness. Of comfort.

"I'll let them report," Manny replies. The door is still open. A wet and bedraggled man walks in, and I recognize him instantly. Uriah. He's alive! My first instinct is happiness – yet another one of my comrades survived the fight. And then I'm angry. Because the last time I saw Uriah, he was abandoning Max on the battlefield in order to save his own skin.

Uriah is beaten. His uniform is in tatters, he is covered in mud and his eyes are red. His gaze meets mine. A relieved smile touches his lips.

I don't return the gesture.

"Lieutenant True," Colonel Rivera says. "Your report?"

He nods, nearly collapsing on the floor. Someone helps him into a chair. He is clearly exhausted and needs medical help. But we need this information *now*.

"I saw...them," he pants, chest heaving. "They were...loading trucks...with prisoners of war."

"Did you see Chris?" I ask, stepping closer. "Uriah? Did you see him?"

"It was hard to see *anything* in this weather," Uriah replies.

"Where were they? Where were *you*?"

19

"I was unconscious in the mud," he says, unflinching. My unspoken accusation hangs heavy in the air: *You left Max to die. You left all of us to die.*

"I was dragging my butt back to camp when I saw the trucks," he continues, never taking his eyes from mine. "They were taking prisoners. Mostly officers. I didn't see Chris, but I would assume that if he was alive, he would be with them."

I take a deep, steadying breath.

So. The possibility remains: Chris *could* be alive.

"Are you *sure*?" Manny presses.

Uriah flicks his darkest, most menacing glare at him.

"I'm *positive.*"

I glance back at Colonel Rivera.

"We have to go after them," I say. "I'll take a platoon up the interstate and we'll stop the trucks."

"We're not stopping anything," Colonel Rivera snaps. "Our forces are in bad shape. We need to regroup and reorganize."

"Chris Young has been taken *captive*!" I reply firmly. "We don't have time to reorganize. We need to act *now.*"

"I will not compromise any more lives for the life of one Commander," Rivera answers, a sour expression on his face. "Regardless of whether or not it's Young or any other officer."

"We need Chris," Manny interjects, keeping his hand on my shoulder. "There's an enormous amount of loyalty to him in the militias, and he's a damned good friend of mine."

"The answer is no," Rivera says.

"You can't sentence him to death!" I yell.

I am furious. Once again, Rivera is denying us help when we need it most.

"We are *all* at risk," he answers gravely. "This is a war."

"We're fighters. We can't just give up."

"I am preserving the men we have left."

"You're *hiding!* We have to go *after* those trucks!"

"We will not." Rivera slams his cigar on the table, color bleeding into his cheeks. "We will regroup and pull back."

Pull back? God, is he insane?

"But we pushed them out!" I counter. "Omega is on the defensive. We've got the initiative, and we should keep pressing."

"Our mission is done." Rivera folds the biggest map. "This discussion is over."

"I won't leave him to die," I say, placing my fists on the table.

"He's probably already dead."

I press my lips together, burning with cold anger.

"You don't want to do this," I warn quietly.

Vera leans forward, frowning. Angela is frozen.

"It's done," Rivera answers.

There is no regret in his voice.

I say nothing. I glare at him, and as he continues folding the maps, I turn around and look at Manny. His expression is difficult to read – then again, my eyes are full of tears, so it's hard to see straight. I push my way through the crowd inside the restaurant – all of them, and me - full of resentment, disappointment and frustration. When I step outside, the cold air is sharp against my cheeks.

I inhale slowly.

Keep it together. Don't let them see you cry.

So I don't.

The old *Jack in the Box* that we've been using as a medical center is packed. Soldiers are crammed into every square inch of space, and the medical staff is working overtime. The building stinks of blood and sweat and pain. I sit on the curb outside the front door, listening to the moans and tortured screams of injured men.

It's horrible. I want to run away and be free of it, but there is nowhere to go.

"I'm sorry, Cassidy."

I raise my head slightly. Uriah is exiting the building. His hand has been bandaged and his wounds have been cleaned. He looks better.

"Sorry for *what?*" I say quietly.

"For what happened to Chris. And Jeff." He swallows. "And Max."

"What happened to Max is your fault," I say simply.

"I didn't leave him behind on purpose," he answers.

"You ran *away*." I stand up. "You abandoned him. All of us."

"I was doing what I had to do to stay alive," he counters.

"This isn't about individual survival, Uriah," I say. "This is about keeping the team alive. We're all a part of the team. Or did you miss one of the three million times Chris pointed this out to us?"

"It was a mistake," Uriah replies, his jaw tight. Dark eyes flashing. "I said I was sorry, and I'm not going to apologize again."

"Good. Don't."

He sighs heavily.

"Look, Cassidy-"

"-That's Lieutenant Hart to you," I snap. "Go get some rest, soldier. You need it." I shove my hands in my pockets and begin to walk away. Uriah catches my shoulder. I push his hand off and turn around, dangerously close to doing something violent. Tears still burn at the edges of my vision, blurring the world.

"I know this is difficult for you," Uriah says, grabbing my shoulders. "I've watched friends die, too. I understand."

I don't move.

"Are you going to let Rivera get away with this?" he whispers.

I raise my chin.

"He's not getting away with anything," I answer.

I take a step back, giving him a warning look. I size him up. He's a good six feet, black wavy hair, olive complexion. A strong soldier and a capable sniper. Maybe he's right. Maybe he *did* just make a mistake in the heat of the battle.

Or maybe not.

But he has a point: Am I going to let Rivera get away with leaving Chris?

No.

"Are Sophia and Derek okay?" I ask.

"They're fine," Uriah replies. "Minor injuries. Nothing compared to what happened to you..." He trails off, sadness in his voice.

I don't want to hear anymore.

"Meet me at D2 at oh-eight-hundred," I state. "Don't be late."

He looks curious. D2 is what we've been calling the empty coffee shop at the edge of the rest area. The D stands for *Dugout*, which was what we used to call the lounge area back at Sector 20, the National Guard Base in Fresno.

He nods. I walk away.

Uriah is right. I'm not going to let Rivera get away with this.

D2 was a nice place, once. The coffee bar is now cracked, patched with spare plywood. Chairs and tables are makeshift or broken. The soldiers that are gathered inside the small building are standing or sitting cross-legged on the floor. There are more here than I expected. Familiar faces. Uriah. Vera. Sophia. Derek. Manny.

Unfamiliar faces, too. New men and women. About thirty in all.

I'm standing on the other side of the bar.

It's dark, cold. A gas lantern glows orange against the far wall.

"Thank you for coming," I say, steadying my voice. Surprisingly, I am not nervous. I am hollow, except for the fiery coals of anger and frustration burning inside of me. Talking to a group of thirty does not scare me: losing Chris scares me *much* more than this. "You may have heard rumors about why I called this meeting." I clear my throat, glance at Manny, and continue. He dips his head slowly, assuring me that I'm doing fine.

"As you know, Commander Young went MIA yesterday," I continue. "According to intelligence reports, he is being taken, along with other militia officers, in Omega trucks. Those trucks are heading south on the interstate. South is where Omega is strongest. The epicenter of their western front is based in Los Angeles."

I pause before continuing.

"Our Commander and several other officers are prisoners of war," I state. "You all know how Omega operates. They capture, interrogate and kill. Colonel Rivera has refused my request to send a rescue unit to stop the trucks and bring them home."

"Why the hell would he do that?" Derek says sharply. He is sitting near Sophia, who is regarding the entire situation with a solemn expression. She has hardly spoken to me since she's returned from the battlefield.

"Because he's a *Colonel*," Manny drawls. "I said it before and I'll say it again: politics. It's all about the *politics*."

"What politics?" Derek demands. "This is a battlefield."

"He's trying to save his own skin and his own men," Manny shrugs. "If the militias fall by the wayside while he does so, it's no skin off his nose."

"But it *is*," I interrupt. "He's just doing what he thinks is right."

I am surprised to hear those words come out of my mouth. Why should I cut Colonel Rivera any slack?

"Look, I didn't call you here so you could argue," I say. "I called you here to ask you a question. I want to bring those men back. Chris Young is the best leader the militia forces have ever had and ever *will* have. I'm asking you to volunteer to join my rescue unit." I take a deep breath before going on. "I have received no authorization from the Colonel and we can expect no support from the Guard. It's dangerous. The chances of all of us coming back alive are slim. But I believe it's worth the risk. We all swore an oath to leave no fighter behind, and I want to uphold that promise."

I look around at the faces in the room. Battle-tested, hardened individuals.

"Who's with me?" I ask.

Manny leans lazily against the wall, raising his hand. I nod at him, holding his gaze in silent thanks.

Uriah lifts his hand, along with Derek. To my shock, Vera raises her hand, as well. The rest of the soldiers don't look so certain. Silence fills the room, and I realize that I need to step up my game.

"Here's the thing," I say, wiping my hands on my jacket. My palms are sweaty. Apparently I *am* nervous. "This is a volunteer mission. Nobody is making you go. Colonel Rivera is pulling our forces out of the Chokepoint tomorrow morning. We'll be back in Fresno by nightfall. If that's what you want to do, go for it. If you're loyal to Chris and the militia and everything that he's fought for, stay here. Help him and the other officers. We *need* Chris. He's one of the biggest reasons we've had so much success as a military force."

"How do we know Chris isn't a traitor, too?" Sophia replies.

I stare at her. Her hands are curled into fists on her knees. A tight, resentful expression lights her dark features.

"What are you saying?" I grit.

"Don't you think it's convenient that at the exact same time that a chunk of our militia betrayed us, Chris conveniently went *missing*?" she accuses. There is no sympathy in her eyes. Only pure, boiling anger. "Who's to say that he didn't orchestrate the entire thing?"

"And I guess he orchestrated Jeff's death, too," I snap. "You don't even know what you're saying."

"I know *exactly* what I'm saying," Sophia replies coldly. "It doesn't add up."

"Chris Young would *die* before he betrayed us," Uriah says, turning his dark gaze on Sophia. "You're a fool to think otherwise."

"There is no one more loyal to the militias than Commander Young," Vera agrees. She glances at me. "Cassidy is right. We need him."

I shake myself. This is a new twist:

Sophia is attacking and Vera is defending me.

What is happening to my world?

"I'm in," a young man says. I remember him. Andrew. Tall and lean, dark hair and a great shot with a rifle. He has always been dependable on the battlefield. I nod, thankful for his support. More than half of the soldiers in the room raise their hands. That's twenty-five.

"This will be considered desertion, you know," Manny interjects. "Going against Rivera's orders...pulling back to track those trucks while he takes the National Guard back to Fresno. He's liable to throw quite a fit."

"We're here on a volunteer basis," I say. "We'll do what we want."

"There will be consequences when we return," Vera points out.

"We'll deal with them."

"You're making a mistake," Sophia presses. "It's not worth any more people dying to go after *one* man."

I swallow a slew of stinging retorts and steady my emotions.

I will deal with my anger at Sophia later.

"This is a war," I say, echoing Colonel Rivera. "People die."

"How are we going to assemble a rescue team without Rivera finding out?" Uriah asks. His gaze is deep, intense. It makes me a little uncomfortable. "He'll go ballistic if he finds out what we're planning."

"He won't find out." I smile slightly. "Our convoy is massive. We'll pull out of line, let the others pass, then turn around and head up the interstate."

"We can't just *drive* into Los Angeles like a bunch of tourists," Derek says.

"We won't." I glance at Manny. "Manny's got connections."

"I will scout ahead," he replies, illustrating a plane in flight with his hands. "It's elementary, really. The fat cats like Rivera head back to Fresno, I go ahead and meet you at a rendezvous point with friendly militia Underground operatives, and you meet me there. Simple, easy and effective." He winks.

"What will we do when we get to the rendezvous point?" Vera asks.

"Manny will arrange transportation to get us into Los Angeles," I say.

"What kind of transportation? If we have vehicles, why not just take those all the way into the city?"

"Because the city is infested with Omega forces," Derek replies. "We won't be able to get close enough without being detected." He looks at me. "Right?"

"Correct," I agree. "And the Underground operatives will have information we'll need to find Chris."

"I thought you were going to track *trucks*," Sophia snorts.

"We are." I give her a stern, warning look. "But remember that those trucks are long gone now, probably already back in Los Angeles. The Underground will know where they would take POWs like Chris."

"Like Chris?"

"High level officers."

I clasp my hands behind my back.

"So," I say, resolved. "We have a plan of action and we have volunteers. All we need is a Commander. I say we take a vote."

Manny laughs.

"It'll be a landslide," he chuckles. "My vote rests on you, my girl."

"So does mine," Uriah says.

"Me too," Derek shrugs.

"But...I'm not a field commander," I say, shocked.

Yes, I am organizing a rescue unit to save Chris, but I am not a commander. Not like him. I'm a Lieutenant. A sniper. I was planning on someone else being in charge.

"You have the battlefield experience we need," Uriah points out. "Besides, we trust you. You've been leading the militias as long as Chris has. And if Chris trusts you, I do, too."

He holds my gaze for a few moments, turning to the others.

"Does anyone here disagree?" he asks.

Silence.

Everyone in the room slowly raises their hands. Manny smiles with satisfaction, almost smug. I lick my lips, fear creeping into my heart.

What have I gotten myself into?

I am no longer a Lieutenant. I am a Commander.

I am in charge. And I'm scared.

Chapter Three

As a child, I spent most of my time alone. I was my own best friend. My daily activities consisted of homework, chores and pretending that I was widely loved and adored by all. And by *all* I mean the collection of toys and stuffed animals I kept in my room. I played with wooden swords and dressed my dolls as commando operatives. I read books about the lives of famous world leaders. People like Alexander the Great, Napoleon Bonaparte and George Washington. I enjoyed history. I liked imagining myself as someone important. Why?

I suppose it was because I was a *nobody*, and I wanted to feel accepted.

Now, as the Commander of a paramilitary rescue unit headed into Los Angeles, I feel more than acceptance. I feel raw fear. I am not afraid that I will die. No. The possibility of death is something I accepted long ago.

I am afraid that I will fail my mission...and fail Chris. Once upon a time Chris took control of a militia group called the *Free Army* to rescue me from an Omega slave labor camp. That group is now called the *Freedom Fighters*, and I am taking them into the heart of Omega's stronghold to save Chris's life.

I don't think I'm ready.

But here I am.

I am sitting in a Humvee. Uriah is in the driver's seat and I am in the passenger side. Despite my anger that he abandoned Max on the battlefield, I must admit that I've appreciated his support. He really *does* seem sorry. People panic in battle. They make bad decisions. And who am I to hold a grudge? I've certainly made plenty of my own mistakes since the collapse.

Vera is in another vehicle with Derek, and Manny…well, he's with his biplane, getting ready to scout ahead and meet us at the rendezvous point in the Tehachapi Mountains. The National Guard convoy is rolling out of Headquarters, a massive movement of trucks and vehicles heading north. It's surreal to watch.

We came. We fought. We won.

For now.

"They'll be back," Uriah mutters.

"Who?" I ask.

"Omega." He adjusts his grip on the steering wheel. "Don't you find it a little hard to believe that they would pull back completely and just let us retreat? They've got a five million-man army. Let's be realistic."

I fold my hands in my lap. The Humvee rumbles to life. Soldiers and officers outside shout orders. Troops are being loaded into transport trucks.

"Something scared them off," I suggest.

Something caused Omega to retreat, and it wasn't the National Guard. Many of our *own* men turned on us. We should still be outnumbered. In fact, we should probably be dead.

So why did Omega break off the attack?

"She's not coming," Uriah states.

I blink, following his line of sight. Sophia is standing near a transport truck headed northbound. She is dressed in uniform, her gear on her back and a rifle on one shoulder. Her short, dark hair is hidden beneath a beanie.

I watch her carefully. Her face has no expression. She looks up, sensing someone watching her, and locks eyes with me. I slowly shake my head.

Don't do this, I think. *We've been through so much together.*

She lifts her chin, pursing her lips. She takes a step onto the bumper below the rear gate of the truck, turns her back, and steps inside. She disappears into the dark maw of the vehicle.

I exhale sharply.

Why is she doing this? After everything that's happened?

"She's grieving," Uriah says, softening. "People in grief do illogical things."

I study his profile. His eyes are trained on the road, soft black hair tangled under a National Guard baseball cap. Since when has Uriah become a friend to me?

"She's angry," I reply. "She blames me for losing Alexander and Jeff."

"That's not your problem. That's hers."

"Sophia has been my friend since we were POWs in a labor camp."

"People change, and sometimes you don't know why." He turns slightly, touching my knee with his hand. "You're better than her, Cassidy. You've got greatness in you."

My mouth goes dry.

"That's *Lieutenant* Hart to you," I murmur.

"Actually, you're a Commander now," he counters.

I don't reply. Chris is the one who offers words of wisdom when I am hurting.

Not Uriah.

"How far away did Manny say the rendezvous point was?" Uriah asks, clearing his throat. Changing the subject. Removing his hand from my knee.

"Three hours, tops, in these trucks," I say. "Manny has friends in the Underground in the Tehachapi Mountains. That's our contact."

"The Colonel's going to be pissed."

"He'll have to deal with it."

Lately, I've been surprised at my own behavior. Recently, stuff that comes out of my mouth is tight and cold. Commanding, even. It's unlike me, and yet...it *is*, somehow.

This isn't who I am. It's just *part* of who I am.

Cassidy Hart, the smart mouthed girl from L.A., died somewhere on the battlefield. At some point, she was replaced by a battle hardened ex-slave laborer and the Lieutenant of a sniper platoon.

Cassidy Hart has changed.

"Here we go," Uriah mutters.

I lean forward, peering ahead. The convoy is moving forward, a mass of transport trucks and commandeered vehicles filling the freeway. The sky is beautiful. The sun is just peeking over the horizon, filling the hills with a gorgeous gold tone.

Uriah gently eases the Humvee onto the freeway. The back of our vehicle is stocked with supplies and weaponry – the other members that volunteered for our rescue unit follow in separate trucks.

The radio on my belt crackles.

"Yankee, this is Sundog," Manny says, his voice scratchy. "I'm ready."

"Roger that, Sundog," I reply, hiding a grin. "Happy flying."

We rumble down the interstate, headed northbound. The speed at which the convoy travels is no more than fifteen to twenty miles per hour – maddeningly slow. Discreetly, Uriah pulls to the right hand side of the road, waving follow-on vehicles ahead.

"You better pray they don't notice this, Commander," Uriah comments.

"They won't," I say. But I'm not confident. I'm bluffing.

Uriah pulls off the road completely and the truck sits there, idling. The convoy continues to pass us by, a roaring collection of engines and troop transports. The truck that Sophia is in lumbers past. A sick, devastated feeling washes over me.

Sophia is angry at the world, my conscious tells me. *Her decisions are her own, and you can't waste time worrying about her. Your job is to keep your team safe and to rescue Chris. Focus on the objective, Cassidy!*

I shake myself, but the sting of Sophia's betrayal is still there.

After everything that's happened in the last week, this is the icing on the cake. I can't deal with it. I don't have the time or energy. So I take my damaged emotions, put them in a box, and throw the box out the figurative window.

It's game time, and nothing will defeat me.

I twist around in my seat, keeping an eye on the convoy. The staging area by the rest stop is slowly emptying of all of its vehicles. The Blackhawk helicopters in the parking lot growl to life, slicing the air with their incredible blades. They rise into the sky, hulking masses that will defend the convoy from the air.

"I almost wish we were going back to Sector 20," Uriah sighs. "At least we'd have some time to recover from all of this."

I keep my mouth shut.

I would love to return to Sector 20, but that's not an option. Not right now.

It takes a *long* time for the last of the convoy to finally fade into the distance. We are four vehicles idling on the side of the road. Two transport trucks and two Humvees. Our rescue unit – the unit that's going to take on the entire Omega contingent.

"Okay, boys," I say into my radio, "Let's roll."

Uriah steps on the gas, steers the Humvee into a tight U-turn, and just like that, we are heading south.

"Will Rivera come after us when they realize we're gone?" Uriah asks.

"No," I say. "It's not worth it to him."

I reach up and touch the gold shield necklace on my chest. A gift from Chris. It seems like he gave it to me such a long time ago, but in actuality, it hasn't even been one year yet.

Things change so quickly.

We drive south on the interstate until we hit the cratered remains of the road destroyed during the fighting. *The Battle of the Grapevine* is what the men are calling it. Landmines and rockets ripped apart most of the concrete, and what the bombs didn't get, Omega's Air Force nailed on their strafing runs.

"There are still some landmines planted out here," I warn Uriah. "This is where we'll be taking the old roads."

"How old, exactly?"

"Don't worry, I know where I'm going." I unfold a map from my bag. It's a military map, full of exact coordinates, latitudes and longitudes. But what we will be using are the back roads, those that will take us to Highway 138. I know from intelligence reports that Omega rarely uses anything but the major interstates like I-5 or Highway 99. Highway 138 will be a safe way to get us where we are going: Lancaster, California.

"I'll already be there before your trucks have made a U-turn," Manny joked earlier.

"You'd better be," I replied. *"Because I don't know who these people are."*

"Relax, my girl. Manny's got it all under control. They're old friends of mine."

*"How old? And exactly what do you mean by **friends**?"*

Manny wiggled his eyebrows, then.

"I mean they're not my enemies, and for the moment that's good enough for me." He paused. *"Are you doing all right, though?"*

I shrugged.

"Chris is gone, Jeff is dead, Alexander is MIA," I said, *"And now I'm the Commander of a suicide mission going to Los Angeles. Everything's great."*

Manny tapped my cheek with one of his long, bony fingers.

"You can do it," he told me cheerfully.

I'm not sure what he meant by *that,* but thinking back on the conversation gives me some peace of mind. Manny believes in me – and even if he *is* slightly eccentric, he's proven himself to be a good soldier and an even better friend.

I trust him.

Sophia, on the other hand…

"This is it," I say, pointing to an off ramp. The mountains rise high into the air, the peaks dusted with snow. Mud and puddles mar the road. Tire tracks zigzag along the potholed highway, an indication of Omega's recent presence.

And on the side of the hills, there is nothing but charred, ashy soot from the battle fires.

"It'll grow back," I whisper.

Uriah gives me a weird look. I ignore it.

It was *my* idea to start a fire to push Omega back. This is the consequence.

I have always loved the beauty of these mountains, and seeing so much of it burned is painful.

Everywhere I go, Omega has caused destruction.

The Tehachapi Mountains are unique. They stretch for about forty miles in the southern quarter of California. There are few pine trees or cedars here. It is mostly grassy hills and land best used for grazing cattle. The terrain is steep. In a few places, trees and shrubbery are thick.

I keep my eye on the three vehicles behind us.

It's an hour drive from the bottom of the Grapevine to the rendezvous point, but it will take us longer because we are traveling slower. We have to keep an eye out for Omega scouts or rogue militia forces. The dangers of traveling without the rest of our convoy are immense. We are on our own.

We are deserters.

For the time being, at least.

Thinking about what we've done brings a sour taste to my mouth. I feel guilty for leaving the National Guard behind, but in my heart I know that this is the right thing to do. It's not just Chris we'll be rescuing if we're successful, anyway. It will be other militia officers that have been captured, too.

"Hey, are you seeing this?" Uriah asks.

I look up from my map.

"Wow."

The sun is hitting the snow-lined peaks just right, creating a prism of light. It's almost heavenly. I admire it for a long time before saying,

"Not everything can be destroyed by Omega."

Uriah nods.

We're on a little known back road that winds through the mountains. We're out in the open, exposed. It makes me nervous. The mountains rise up on each side of us as we roll into a small grazing valley. Broken cattle fences line the side of the road. Two ranch houses stand in the distance. It's hard to tell, but it looks like they've been burned from the inside out.

An accident? Probably not.

"I don't know Manny as well as you do," Uriah says quietly. "I hope you trust him enough to believe in his friends."

"Manny is a good soldier," I reply simply. "He knows what he's doing."

Most of the time.

Uriah doesn't look too sure. It doesn't make me any more confident about my decision.

Why did they have to vote me Commander? I think angrily. *I don't want to be in charge. I just want to rescue Chris.*

I'm not a leader. I'm *not*.

After forty-five minutes of driving, the mountains loom closer, crowding the road. The trees are thicker here.

"We're almost there," I say. I look at the map. "There should be some kind of a basin coming up. It looks like a lake."

"You mean *that*?" Uriah tips his head.

I stare at a huge hole in the ground. There is no water left. Only mud and sludge, an aftereffect of the heavy rain.

"Yeah, *that*," I reply.

I scan the landscape. The road begins to climb upward, winding around the base of a huge mountain. We grind onto a gravel access road for a good half hour. I keep my eyes trained on the road, trying to avoid thoughts of ambush.

The pain of being separated from Chris is physical. Like a knife in the chest.

Please, God, I pray. *Let him be alive.*

"Whoa," Uriah says.

We come to a straightaway in the road. It flattens suddenly and we're pulling into a wide-open space, surrounded on all sides by thick trees and foliage. At the end of the road is a ranch house; similar to the ones I've seen on the way here. The house is old and big. Several outbuildings sit nearby We come to metal pole gate, topped with coils of wicked barbed wire. There are sand-bagged fortifications to our right and left. Four German Shepherds run the perimeter of the inside of the fence, barking and growling viciously.

A metal sign on the gate reads:

PRIVATE PROPERTY:

TRESPASSERS WILL BE SHOT.

Uriah kills the engine. The other trucks follow our lead. I open the passenger door, step outside, and breathe in the crisp mountain air. I grab my rifle and sling it over my shoulder, keeping it close.

"This isn't what I had in mind," Andrew says.

He files out of the back of one of the transport trucks, his gear on his back.

"What were you picturing?" Vera snaps, slamming the door to her Humvee. "The freaking Taj Mahal?"

I give her a look.

She rolls her eyes, twisting her hair into a tight ponytail. I'm surprised she doesn't rip it out. But her eyes are watchful, fierce.

"Where's Manny?" Derek asks.

"He's here," I assure him.

"Where do we go in?" Vera says. "How do we know this place is safe?"

"Manny should be-" I begin, but I stop. "We're being watched."

"Obviously," Vera replies. "We're surrounded."

Well, duh. My men watch the sides of the road carefully. Several armed guards emerge from the foliage, well camouflaged and silent. They wear no uniforms. In fact, they are dressed as civilians. But they are armed, and that is enough.

"National Guard," I say. "I'm Yankee One. We're with Manny."

"Yes, I know." A slender, almost-invisible figure emerges from the woods. It's a woman. She's tall, white-haired. A green shirt is tucked into her combat pants. A pattern of soft wrinkles frames her pretty face.

A German Shepherd darts out of the bushes and streaks toward me.

I instinctively take a defensive stance and bring my rifle up, ready to smash the stock of the weapon into the dog's face when it bites. And I realize something in that moment: I'm not afraid of the dog. I'm not afraid of being bitten.

I'm just reacting to a threat like a robot.

I really *have* changed.

"Cinco, no!" the woman says.

She rushes forward. The dog hesitates when it hears her command, and it pulls back, but it continues to growl, circling me. The woman grabs the dog by the collar, dragging it backward as much as she can manage, sternly telling it to stand down.

"I'm sorry," she says, offering a halfhearted grin. "Cinco's just doing her job."

"I can respect that," I remark.

"Welcome to Safe Zone One," the woman keeps a hand on Cinco's collar. The dog is still growling menacingly. "Is this it?"

"Is what it?" Vera snaps.

"Is this your entire rescue unit?"

"Yeah." The small size of the unit must be disappointing. "We pack a mean punch."

Arlene's eyes soften a bit.

"I believe you," she answers.

"We don't have a lot of time," I say. "We need to get moving as soon as possible. Do you have everything we need?"

"I will." She looks over her shoulder, whistling shrilly.

As I turn and open the lead Humvee's back door, Manny comes out of the woods. His flight cap is stuffed into the pocket of his duster. He's flushed. It looks like he's been running.

"Manny?" I say. "Are you okay?"

"Never been better," he replies, bending down. Scratching Cinco behind the ears. "I see you made it in one piece. That's good news."

"You could say that," Vera remarks.

"It wasn't as bad as we thought it'd be," I shrug.

He bats the dog's tail away.

"I told you it was purely elementary, didn't I?"

"Let's go inside," I say, reminding myself that *I'm* in charge, and therefore *I* should lead the way. "Standing around in the open isn't wise."

The hills could have eyes other than our own.

"Good call," Andrew murmurs.

Vera gives him a condescending look as she passes him.

Why is she even here? I wonder. *It's certainly not because she's my biggest fan.*

I lead the platoon – about twenty-five people in all – to the front of the gate. The woman falls into step beside me, Manny on her left. The dog is silent. I keep my eye on it, regardless.

"I'm Arlene, by the way," the woman says. "Codename Shepherd One on the radio."

Ironic.

"You've got a reputation, Cassidy," she continues

"So I've been told," I answer.

She unlocks the gate, shouting at the powerful guard dogs on the other side, commanding them to be silent. They cease most of the barking and growling, prowling around the sides of the fence. They know their master, and they have been trained to respond well.

Manny says something to Arlene in a low voice.

She playfully slaps his shoulder. He laughs good-naturedly.

Hmm.

The front walkway to the ranch house is wide, packed tight with gravel, the lawn perfectly manicured. The house itself is three stories, painted in muted earth tones, blending in with

44

the terrain. A sprawling bunkhouse sits on the right hand side of the property, and in the back, there are stables and corrals.

"Nice place," Vera comments.

"Yes," Arlene replies. "Been in the family for generations."

We reach the front door. It's huge, oak and bracketed with black iron hinges. Arlene pushes it open and we step inside. I take a deep breath, marveling at the 19th century design. Large windows in the second floor shed natural light into the room. It smells like aged leather and dusty books. And food! Something is cooking, and the scent is mouthwatering.

How long has it been since I've been inside a *house*?

"Welcome to the Double Y Ranch," Arlene announces, standing at the end of the entryway. "We're a way-station for traveling soldiers and a proud thorn in the side of Omega. What you see and hear in this place is confidential. We are a low-profile operation, and I expect you to all to treat this location accordingly."

I nod.

"How long have you been working with the Underground?" I ask.

"Since the beginning," she replies. She glances at Manny. "I'll be able to help you reach Los Angeles. Up until this point, I haven't been told what your mission is, and I won't ask."

"This is a rescue unit," I explain briefly.

"Ah, so it's true, then," she frowns. "Commander Young was captured."

I hold her gaze. Yes. It's true.

"Commander, you have my word," she says, "that I will do everything in my power to help you and your men pull off a successful mission."

I find myself smiling.

"Thank you," I reply.

And I mean it. From the bottom of my heart.

Chapter Four

Here's the thing that nobody tells you about being in love:
It's hard.

Anything good in life takes work, and lately, a lot of blood,
sweat and tears. My relationship with Chris Young has always
been defined not just by mutual attraction, but by the fact that
we were brought together in the middle of a post-apocalyptic
warzone.

Flowers and dinner dates? Never had those.

Firefights and battle fatigue? That's more like it.

Wartime hardship has always been the dominating factor
in our romance. It's what brought us together, it's what's *kept*
us together, and now...it's what has torn us apart. Being
separated from Chris is more difficult for me than being
separated from my father. Because through *everything*, Chris
has been the one that has kept my feet on the ground. He's
been the one to protect me, train me, and teach me how to
survive. The fact that I'm still alive is a testament to *his*
skillset, not mine.

And not knowing if he's alive or dead is killing me.

Our platoon is gathered at the long table in the dining
room of Arlene's ranch house. Derek is sitting across from me.
Vera is on my left, Uriah is on my right, and Manny and Arlene
are seated on the other end of the table. Andrew is sitting on a
couch, fiddling with a radio.

"The plan?" Manny echoes. "We eat."

Several women pop out of the kitchen, serving us food. Someone sets a bowl of steaming beef stew in front of me. It smells fabulous. Much better than the wartime rations I've been eating on the battlefield.

"Where do all these people come from?" I wonder aloud.

"They're refugees," Arlene explains. "They stay here, and in exchange for safekeeping, they help Underground operations run smoothly." She gestures to the soup. "Feeding our soldiers is an important part of that."

"Are you associated with any *specific* militia?" Vera presses.

"I'm a free agent. What I do is here is my own business, and I've chosen to help *all* of the militias." Arlene picks up her spoon. "We've all got to do our part to keep Omega out of our homes."

True words.

"How do you know Manny?" I ask, pointblank.

Arlene seems startled by my question, then takes a bite of stew.

"I've known Manny for many years," she replies.

"Arlene and I go back a *long* time," Manny says.

"Commander," she says, looking at me, "as soon as your men have eaten, I'll give you all the information and equipment you'll need to reach Los Angeles."

I pick up my utensils.

"Has Omega ever showed up on your front doorstep?" Uriah asks. "I mean, every nice ranch house or mansion from here to the valley has pretty much been burned or ripped apart."

"They've yet to find me," Arlene says. "This property is well hidden, far away from the main highways and difficult to spot from the air. Local militia keeps Omega from wandering too far into these hills with harassing fire. I've never had this many militiamen at Double Y before. The sooner you're on your way, the better."

Okay, then.

"What's left of Los Angeles?" Vera suddenly asks.

I flick my gaze to Arlene, watching her face. She frowns slightly, swallows, and answers, "It's different."

"Define different."

"The Port of Los Angeles is being used to receive ships filled with Chinese soldiers," Arlene replies. "Downtown Los Angeles has been commandeered by military units and Beverly Hills has been taken over by high level Omega officers."

"What about the population?" Derek says. "The civilians?"

"They're dead," Arlene answers. No hesitation. "The chemical weapon was...*effective*. The population that remains exists only because Omega has allowed for a labor force. It is entirely a military city. A fortress."

"The militias and the National Guard stopped Omega's northward push into the valley," I say. "I don't think it was because we had more soldiers or firepower. Something drove them back, and it wasn't us. Has something happened that we need to know about?"

"She's a smart one," Manny tells Arlene. "Or didn't I tell you that already?"

"You've told me," Arlene says. "Eat your dinner. I'll explain everything afterward. I promise."

I can live with that.

"We're walking into a hellhole," Vera mutters to me. "Once we go into Los Angeles, there's no coming out."

"I told you upfront that this was no picnic," I reply, sharp. "If you're worried, stay here. I don't care."

And I really don't.

I don't need Vera Wright any more than I need a diamond ring at this point.

She glares at me, and once again I wonder why she's here.

For Chris? Because she's got a crush on him? No. To go on a suicide mission into the heart of an Omega stronghold with a girl that you can't stand requires more than a simple crush as motivation.

What does Vera Wright want from me?

"Tell me, Commander," Arlene inquires, "how long you've been fighting with the militias."

"Chris Young liberated me from an Omega POW camp," I reply. "I joined at that point."

"They say that you're an excellent sniper," she grins.

I take a sip of water. "They've said a lot of things."

"It seems the story of Chris Young and Cassidy Hart has become prime entertainment for members of different militias across the state – and even across the country."

It could be worse.

When we're done eating, I follow Arlene into the living room. She pulls down a map from a floor-to-ceiling bookcase at the end of the room. The room is illuminated with 19th century oil lamps. I stand with my arms crossed, studying the map.

"This is us," Arlene says. She points to a region behind Highway 138, burrowed into the mountains. "You need to get *here*." She drags her finger across the mountains and to the edge of Los Angeles. "Then to the city of Westwood, California. According to Underground operatives, Omega is housing prisoners of war in the Los Angeles County Jail."

My heart sinks.

My father was a Los Angeles cop. I drove by the County Jail many times. It's a fortress.

"Don't look too discouraged, my girl," Manny grins, patting my shoulder. "You don't have to worry about the jail. They're keeping militia *officers* in an entirely different location. Large prisons are too complex and crowded, with limited electricity. But smaller buildings? That's where they keep the important officers."

"Chances are, if Commander Young is still alive," Arlene interjects, "he'll be kept somewhere in downtown Westwood. It's near where many of the ranking Omega officers are encamped, which makes him easily accessible for interrogation."

"Where is the location of this building, exactly?" Uriah asks.

"That I can't say," she shrugs. "Scouts will have more information for you when you reach the Way Houses."

"Say *what?*" Derek demands. "This is too complicated. Give it to us straight and simple, lady."

"Derek," I warn.

But I don't disagree.

"I want the whole story," I say, facing Arlene. "Before we leave here, I want to know everything that you know about Los Angeles."

Manny chuckles, sitting on the couch, propping his legs up on the coffee table.

"I'd say that's a fair deal," he remarks. "What do you say, Arlene?"

She raises an eyebrow.

"Fine," she replies.

And that's when she tells us.

———————————

"Omega was attacked in San Diego," Arlene says.

The room goes silent. Like a tomb.

"By who?" Vera breathes. "United States military?"

"Mexico," Arlene answers.

"*Mexico?*" Derek repeats. "Does Mexico still exist?"

"All I know is what I've heard," Arlene says, raising her hands. "They say that Mexico forces en masse attacked Omega in San Diego. It was huge. Omega was taken by surprise."

"When?" Uriah asks.

"Just a few days ago." Arlene points to the map. "Which is why so many of Omega's forces retreated from the Valley Chokepoint, Commander Hart. Your instincts were correct."

I run a hand through my hair.

"Does this mean Mexico is strong enough to actually help us win this thing?" I ask.

"I have no idea what Mexico's situation is," Arlene says. "But thank God for their help. There are rumors of forces attacking Omega in Washington and Oregon, as well."

"Who would *that* be?" Andrew comments. He's still fiddling with the radio, wires strung across his lap. "Mexico is in the south. Who's up north?"

"Canada," Uriah suggests.

"Are you saying that we've got allies?" I breathe.

"What's she's saying is that *someone*, out of self-preservation, is attacking Omega, too," Manny interrupts. "Which means we're not bearing the full weight of their attacks."

Thank God.

Seriously.

"Which means it might provide the little bit of daylight you need to get your rescue unit into Los Angeles," Arlene adds. "Omega is rolling south to defend their position in San Diego, and from what we've heard, they've got their hands full."

A sign of weakness? A flood of hope rushes over me. Omega is struggling more than I thought they were.

Finally, some good news.

"We have transportation that will enable you to get into the city without being detected," Arlene says. "Underground hotspots are everywhere. There is a Way House where you will meet scouts at the edge of Toluca Lake, not far outside of

Westwood. They will give you the location of the facility where they are holding Commander Young." She traces a circle around the ranch house on the map. "It's about sixty miles from here to Westwood."

"What's a Way House?" Andrew asks, never looking up from his radio.

"A safe place for traveling militiamen to stay," Arlene explains. "Manny will be your guide into the city, considering the mode of transportation that you'll be taking."

"Wait, hold it," Derek says. "We're *not* flying to Los Angeles. That's impossible. Omega's got aircraft everywhere."

"I didn't say we were flying," Manny answers, leaning forward. He grabs a glass dish on the coffee table. It's full of pine nuts. "Although I would *prefer* to fly."

"Then how are we going in?" Vera demands, annoyed.

"You'll see," Manny says.

He's right.

We do.

Chapter Five

"Cassidy, listen to me," Chris says. "If I die fighting, I want you to stay safe. Do you understand?"

"Everything's going to be fine. It always is," I reply, smiling faintly.

"Not this time." He seems desperate to make me believe that this is the end. That we're all going to die, and that I need to brace myself for it. "Cassie. I...need you to promise me that you'll take care of yourself if I'm not here to help you. Make wise decisions. Do what I would do."

"I'm not you," I shrug. "And what's with all the doom and gloom talk? You're Mr. Motivation, remember?"

He grabs my shoulders. Presses a fierce, hot kiss to my lips. I wrap my arms around his neck, stroking his cheek with my thumb. His heart is beating fast.

"What's wrong, Chris?" I whisper. "This isn't like you."

I study his eyes. They're tinged with red. From stress? From physical exhaustion? Probably a combination of both. But it's unlike him to voice concerns like this out loud.

"I just need you to promise me that if I die," he says, "you'll go back to Camp Freedom. Find your father. He'll protect you. Can you promise me that?"

"You're not going to die," I state firmly. "And neither am I."

"Cassidy. Promise me."

His gaze is intense.

I drop my eyes, studying the stitching on the collar of his uniform jacket.

"I can't make a promise that I won't keep," I reply. "I can't lie to you."

He brushes his lips across my forehead, fingering my hair.

"Please," he says. His voice breaks.

I close my eyes.

"I promise," I say.

I hate breaking promises. I promised him that if he were to die on the battlefield, I would go back to the mountains and live with Dad. Fortunately, I've got a keen eye for loopholes. Chris didn't *die* on the battlefield. He went missing in action.

There's a difference.

So here I am, leading a rescue unit into Los Angeles.

Sorry, Chris. I love you too much to leave you in the hands of my enemies.

Even if it means breaking my promise?

Yes. Even then.

I'm sitting on the edge of the biggest couch in the living room of the ranch house. We are leaving tonight. It's cold, drizzly and dark. I stare out the front window. I have barely been able to rest while I've been here. I'm anxious, on edge. Wondering where Chris is...if he's alive...if he's being interrogated. What if he's being tortured?

I can't even *think* about that.

I stand up and pace the length of the room, boots sinking into the soft carpet. The platoon is outside, getting ready. I'm waiting for my Lieutenants to meet me here. I need to speak to them privately before we leave this place.

Because when we leave...we might not be coming back.

Morbid, but true.

"What's up, boss?" Derek asks as he saunters into the room, his rifle over his shoulder, pack on his back. "Bad news?"

"No," I reply.

Uriah, Vera, and Andrew enter the room right behind him, geared up and ready to go.

"You're going to need to travel as lightly as possible," I say. "We're not driving into Los Angeles, it's too dangerous. And we can't fly, either."

"So how are we getting *in*, Hart?" Vera snaps. "We can't just appear there."

"I'll show you," I say.

We take a long hallway toward the back of the building, exiting into the backyard. Only *this* backyard is massive. An empty swimming pool fed by a natural spring is wedged between lavish landscaping – exotic shrubbery and marble water fountains.

"Geez *Louise*," Derek says. "How rich *was* Arlene?"

"Very rich," Manny replies. "Her family raised cattle for over a hundred years. Good salt-of-the-earth people."

"How do you know her family?" I ask.

"We go back a long way. I'll tell you the story sometime."

"Fair enough."

In the back of the property, the stables stand tall and proud. The building is beautiful, and once we enter the side door, I smell straw and livestock. It's a comforting scent. One that reminds me of my time spent with Chris and his family last Christmas. Before their farm was burned to the ground.

The interior is glowing with lamplight. Beautiful horses snort and shake their heads in their stalls. Maybe they're not used to having this many people in their living space.

Sorry, guys.

"Oh, my God..." Vera mutters. "Horses. We're taking horses."

"It's the tactical edge we need," Manny exclaims. "And fortunately for you, I know everything there is to know about horseback riding. You're welcome."

"We're going to die on these things," Vera sighs.

"Not likely," I reply. "United States Special Forces used horses in Afghanistan. They're tough, they make good time, they're pretty much all-terrain...and they'll get us in and out of the city undetected."

"Not a bad idea," Andrew remarks.

"Not bad at all," Uriah adds.

Vera slowly, hesitantly strokes the nose of a toffee-colored horse. She's smiling, peaceful. When she catches me watching her, she hardens.

"So," she says. "What now?"

"We saddle up, obviously," Manny replies. He pats the cheek of a brown-hued horse. "Take only the necessary items. Weapons, food, ammo and water. You've all got tactical medical kits on your person, so besides that...you should be set. Keep it light, boys and girls."

"We brought a ton of supplies in the Humvees," Derek comments, "and there's no way we're going to be able to take all of it on horseback. My RPG is going to have to stay behind."

He looks utterly crushed.

"It'll be okay, Derek," I say, squeezing his shoulder. "We can't use an RPG in downtown Los Angeles, anyway. It's not exactly discreet."

"No." He grins. "But it would be *awesome*."

"Manny," I say in a low voice, "you're going to have to walk me through this. I've never been on a horse before."

"Girl, believe me when I say that *you* more than anyone else here is capable of riding a horse," Manny answers. He presses my hand against the forehead of his horse. "This is Katana. She's my favorite of the lot, and the most even-tempered. She's best suited for you."

"Oh." I peek around the side of Katana's head, studying her huge, long lashed brown eyes. "Hey, girl. Nice to meet you."

Katana nickers a soft, breathy nuzzle in response.

"The secret of horseback riding is simple," Manny begins. Arlene strides into the room with a bucket of water, sets it down near Katana's stall, and looks at me.

"I see you've taken a liking to my favorite girl," she whispers.

I shrug. "Um, actually..."

"Ladies," Manny interrupts. "If you don't *mind*, I'm *trying* to give a lecture here."

"Please continue," I say.

The platoon fills the stable. We must look odd. Twenty-five camouflaged militiamen inside a 150-year-old stable. Then again...soldiers and horses were the equivalent to soldiers and Humvees not so long ago.

"Like I was saying before I was interrupted," Manny goes on, raising an annoyed eyebrow, "the secret of horseback riding is very simple. Get on, hang on and pay attention. You exercise common sense and the horse will, too. You stay calm, and the horse will stay calm. You take care of your horse, and your horse will take care of you. It's not really any different than a relationship with a human, actually." He gestures to Katana. "Take this horse, for example. Fine tempered creature, common sense. As long as you treat her right, she'll treat you right."

"Sounds like dating advice to me," Derek remarks.

The militiamen laugh. Manny cracks a smile.

"Very true," Manny says. "Like I said. They're not so different from people."

"How do you know so much about horses, flyboy?" somebody shouts.

"I was raised with horses. Worked with them all my life in a stable before I got into flying. Now who's ready to ride into Los Angeles?"

"Hi-ho Silver," Uriah mutters, smiling at me.

"The Lone Ranger," I say.

"Yeah. Now *that's* a great old show."

I tilt my head. Somehow, Uriah doesn't strike me as someone who would appreciate the classics, but hey. Who am I to judge?

"These horses can go about fifteen to thirty miles in a day with pack loads, provided we give them the proper amount of rest and care on the way into the city," Manny continues. "We'll be traveling on rising and falling terrain, so we'll need to be careful about pushing them too hard." He pauses. "So. Any questions?"

"I got one," Uriah says.

"Go."

He leans against the wall, jerking his thumb at a horse.

"How do we actually ride these things?"

Manny cracks his knuckles and rolls up his sleeves. He looks a little mischievous.

"Now *that*, my boy, is the fun part," he says.

The night is cold, but the clouds have cleared enough to shed white, brilliant moonlight across the mountains. I'm sitting with my boots in the stirrups of Katana's saddle, holding her reins in the palm of my hand. I've got nothing but my rifle on my back, my sidearm on my thigh, my knife on my belt and a jacket buttoned up to the neck.

The horses are snorting blasts of steaming breath in the chill. A couple of them paw the ground.

Manny is seated on a horse beside me, lazily studying his flight cap.

"Are you going to bring that?" I ask.

He looks up. "Of course," he replies. "It's my good luck charm."

"I don't believe in luck."

"You don't, eh? Then what *do* you believe in, Commander?"

I don't answer. Because I'm not sure I know anymore.

I can feel Katana's lungs expand and shrink with each breath. Her body is warm, and every once in a while she snorts through her nose – loudly. Derek is loading up the last of the horses with gear, while the rest of the platoon finds their own animal.

"You have all of the information you'll need," Arlene says. She pats Katana's nose. "Do you have any questions, Commander?"

"No," I reply. "Manny?"

"I'm fine and dandy," he replies. "Not much else to say."

"Good luck, Manny," she says softly. "Come back safely." She looks at me. "You too. I pray that your operation will be successful."

"Thank you," I answer. "We'll be back. Count on it."

"Your mission codename," she says. "What is it? What do I tell the Underground?"

I think about it.

"Angel Pursuit," I say at last.

She nods, approving.

I tap the heels of my boots against Katana's flanks and she moves forward.

Easy enough, I think. *For now.*

The motion of the horse is almost like riding on the moving deck of a ship. Every movement of the animal rolls your body slightly forward and backward. I feel exposed sitting on top of such a big creature. I can see clearly in all directions, but as a mountain fighter, I'm used to traveling within the cover of ravines, behind trees and through bushes. Not perched on top of a twelve-hundred pound horse.

Behind the stables, there's a hidden trail that winds into the woods. Manny moves toward it – but not before he whispers something to Arlene. She smiles.

It's a sad smile. A wistful one.

I wonder what he said.

"Alrighty, Commander," Manny tells me. "I'll lead the way."

"Roger that."

He turns on his horse to look over the platoon. They're saddled up and ready to go. Half of the group looks unsure of what they're doing on their horses, while the other half seems to be adjusting just fine. Uriah is one of the latter.

He trots up beside me, an expression of wry amusement on his face.

"You look pretty relaxed in the saddle," he comments.

I pull back on the reins and turn Katana to the right. I click my tongue against the roof of my mouth and urge her forward. She follows Manny's lead, and the entire platoon begins moving out of the stable area, into the woods.

I frequently look over my shoulder, watching the militiamen. A few of them nearly fall off their horses at first. It's comical to watch – if not a little depressing. My platoon

Lieutenants – Vera, Derek, Andrew and Uriah – adjust the quickest. Unsurprising.

Vera looks royally ticked off to be riding a horse, however, judging by the sour expression on her face. I guess she'd rather take a Humvee into Los Angeles.

So would I, but hey.

There's a war going on.

For the first hour of riding, I find myself adjusting to the sensation of horseback riding. At first it feels odd. Like I'm bouncing – floating. And then I settle into the saddle and relax into the rhythm of Katana's strides. It's nice not to have to hike on foot. But I can't let my guard down. These hills are crawling with rogue militia groups and breakaway gangs that fled the city.

At least that's what I've been told.

According to intelligence reports from the National Guard, Los Angeles is a hotbed of Omega activity – and the ring around the outside of the city limits is a dangerous barrier of violent people.

"Generally speaking," Arlene said earlier, *"Los Angeles is the castle, and the territory outside it is the village. The people that have been locked out of the castle are the few survivors, and the some of them have formed gangs. They're dangerous. Several have created militia groups – only they're rogue. They're not fighting just Omega. They're fighting **anyone**."*

Survival of the fittest.

The mountain trail gently slopes downward, winding between trees and bushes. But as the hours pass, the trail travels up and down and around the hills. At one point, we break the cover of the trees and hit the open, rolling hillside. Grazing territory for cattle.

"We'll want to steer clear of the ridgeline," Manny advises. "Ride the crest just below the top. We don't want to silhouette against the moonlight."

I can't argue with that.

We stick to the trails and stay just enough below the ridgeline to avoid detection, but high enough to get a good view of the surrounding area. A bone-chilling breeze sweeps up the side of the hill, creating a ripple in the grass. I shiver and scan the horizon. It's so open. So *exposed*. I don't like it. I've come to love the cover and concealment of the deep forest.

We come to a spot in the ridge where it becomes necessary for us to deviate from traveling higher. The mountain is divided here. We will have to climb down and then back up.

"Let's get this over with," I breathe. "The sooner we get back on the ridgeline, the better."

"No argument there, Commander," Manny agrees.

So we take our horses downward to the valleys between the mountains. Going downhill on a steep trail is a new experience for me. I almost have to stand in the stirrups, pulling back on the reins. Katana nearly slides to the bottom, sticking her front legs out in front of her, crouching with her hind legs. I nearly topple over her head, but grab the saddle horn to keep myself mounted.

"Have you noticed something?" Uriah asks, hanging onto his mount tightly.

His horse, Mach, is midnight black. It matches Uriah's personality perfectly.

"What are you talking about?" I say.

"I'm talking about *you*." He wraps the reins in his right hand. "This platoon. Notice how everyone is following your orders? You're a great Commander."

"Uriah," I sigh. "I'm *not*. Ordering people around doesn't define a leader. Doing the right thing at the hardest time does."

I'm quoting Chris.

"You want to lead people?" he said one day, long before we ever joined the National Guard. Or before I was even enslaved in a labor camp. *"The key to being a good leader is to make decisions based on facts, not on anger or fear. Find the genius in everyone you work with. Be humble. Don't take credit for victory. It belongs to the group. But the hardest thing about being a leader is doing what you* **know** *in your gut is right. So many times, the simplest answer is the right answer. In the heat of the moment, complex strategies aren't usually the answer. Look for that clear, easy solution. "*

How did he know this? What did he do as a Navy SEAL that gave him such an enormous amount of insight and knowledge? That kind of discernment is rare. And it reminds me that no matter how much I love Chris, there is a *lot* that I don't know about him.

"Hey, Commander," Uriah whispers, snapping me out of it. "Lighten up. You're doing good. Give yourself props."

I raise an eyebrow.

"I don't think patting myself on the back is a good idea," I murmur.

Because honestly, good things don't last.

"Hold up," Manny says, making a closed fist to halt. "We need to let the horses rest and get them some water."

I pull back on Katana's reins and we come to a halt. I dismount and hit the ground.

Dang. My butt is sore.

My thighs ache. I walk stiffly for a few minutes. Now I know why they say cowboys walked bowlegged. The rest of the platoon does the same. More than a few moans and complaints are expressed. We allow the horses to drink water, and while they rest, I study Katana's face. She's a gorgeous animal. Her eyes are full of intelligence and understanding.

"You're a good girl, aren't you?" I whisper. "Yes, you are..."

"I knew it," Manny says.

"What?"

"You're a horse whisperer."

I laugh for the first time in...well, a while.

"She *is* a woman of many talents," Uriah says. His smile is gentle and unguarded. And for some reason that bothers me. He shouldn't be smiling at me like that.

"We barely covered six miles," Vera complains.

"It's better than walking," I say.

"It's slow. And we have to rest these things and water them."

"They're *horses*, Vera." I snap. 'They're carrying you *and* pack loads. Would you rather walk?"

"I'd rather drive or fly."

"That's not an option and you know it."

A muscle ticks in her jaw.

"The horses were *your* idea," she hisses in a low voice. "If Chris is dead by the time we reach him, it will be your fault."

I jerk backward like I've been slapped in the face.

"If we die out here-" she says, but I cut her off.

"-If we *die*," I retort, "we will have died fighting for something *worth* dying for. I'd rather die than take the coward's way out."

"So you're calling me a coward."

"I'm not calling you anything. I'm stating a fact." I take a step back. "This isn't about politics or emotions, Vera. This is about doing the right thing and having the guts to follow through with it." I hold my open palms up. "Either you've got it in you or you don't. Honestly, I really hope that you *do*."

I turn away, not bothering to gauge her reaction. She stands there in silence, staring at the back of my head for a long while before walking away, slowly. I press my cheek against Katana's neck and steady my emotions.

I can do this. I can handle Vera. I can handle *anything*.

Right?

I take a deep breath, feeling another set of eyes on me. Uriah. His expression is pensive as he approaches. He stands a few feet away, silent. It's not awkward, but it's not comfortable, either.

"Cassidy...?" he asks. "What did you *do* before the collapse?"

I cock my head. What *is* this? Are people taking numbers to talk to me?

"Why?" I say.

"I'm just curious. You seem...almost prepped for this lifestyle."

"I was living in Los Angeles," I reply.

"So you'll be going home for the first time when we reach the city."

I swallow. I hadn't thought of it like that, but yes. I'll be seeing the ravaged remains of my former hometown for the first time. I'm not sure that it's going to do anything to boost my confidence. From what I've heard, Los Angeles is little more than an oversized garbage dump these days.

Not really positive reinforcement.

"What kind of a job did you have?" Uriah presses.

I scratch Katana behind the ears. And then I decide not to answer Uriah. Call me crazy, but I'd rather nobody but Chris Young know the details of my past life. My *normal* life. I don't want to burst anyone's illusion that I'm a hardcore freedom fighter by letting the cat out of the bag: *Yes, sorry folks. But Cassidy Hart was an unemployed college dropout before the EMP hit, not a police officer or a soldier. My worst worries were awkward family reunions and failed cell signals. Does that surprise you?*

It's like they say. Leaving an element of mystery is sometimes more effective than spilling your guts everywhere you go. Just saying.

Uriah realizes that I'm not going to answer his question, and instead of pressuring me, he drops the subject. He leans close to my face and whispers,

"Keeping secrets? I can keep them, too."

He presses a soft, quick kiss to my cheek. It happens in a second, just quick enough for everyone else to miss it. I shove him backwards, shocked. He looks taken aback by my reaction. My knife flashes off my belt and into my hand.

"Don't *ever* do that again," I warn quietly, the blade glinting in the moonlight.

Uriah looks shocked by my reaction – and I'm a little bit surprised, too.

My instinct to fight – to defend when threatened – is stronger than it ever was. It surprises me how easily it becomes visible when I am attacked.

"Uh...I'm...sorry..." Uriah mutters, flushed. He slowly backs away, retreating into the shadows of the night, taking refuge on the other side of Mach.

I think, *What does he want from me?*

Yet there's a small part of me that thinks Uriah doesn't want anything. That perhaps he really *does* genuinely care about me. And for some reason, that is scarier than thinking that he's trying to manipulate my emotions.

I love Chris. I will always love Chris. That will never change.

Period.

I can feel the intensity of Uriah's gaze on the back of my head. It's practically drilling holes through my skull. I don't like it. I move to the other side of Katana, casting a glance at Vera. She's sulking as she checks her saddle, but in hindsight, our confrontation could have been a lot worse. In fact, compared to other conversations we've had, what happened could be considered almost civil.

After we rest the horses, we mount up again and continue our journey. I send Uriah to the back of the group. My plan is to make him eat dust for a few hours. Maybe it will force him to think about the consequences of his stupid, rash action.

And the more I think about it, the more annoyed I become.

If Chris were here, he would teach Uriah a few things about manners...

A flicker of movement catches the corner of my left eye. "Whoa, hold it," I say, jerking back on Katana's reins.

We halt and Manny stops, too. He turns back to face me, alarmed. "What?" he demands.

"I saw something move," I reply, nodding toward the spot.

I look toward the tall grass on the side of the mountain. The moonlight casts a silvery glow over the field. In the distance is a decrepit barn. But right below it...I saw something move. And because I'm a sniper, the *possibility* of movement is as problematic as the *confirmation* of it.

"Where?" Manny asks.

"On your nine o'clock," I whisper.

"Roger that, Cassidy," Derek says.

I quickly scan our surroundings. There's nothing but wide-open grassy fields behind us and in front of us. We won't hit a covered area until we reach the base of the next hill. We're completely, totally exposed on our flanks, except for a few rocks and defilades – low spots in the terrain.

It turns my blood to ice water.

This is a kill zone.

"What do we do, boss?" Derek asks me.

*What would Chris do? What would he **say**?*

"We keep going," I say. "Dismount and gun walk to cover."

As soon as the words are out of my mouth, the sound of rifle fire cracks the silence of the night. Behind me, a horse rears on its hind legs, whinnying loudly. The militiaman on his back – a man named Matt – is thrown to the ground. He flies through the air like a limp ragdoll, landing with a sickening *crunch* on his neck. I drop out of my saddle and crouch on the protected side of Katana's shoulder. I spring to the man on the ground. His head is twisted at an unnatural angle, his eyes wide open.

Dead.

And there's a red bullet wound right below his ear.

"Ambush!" I shout. "Cover, cover, cover!"

Whoever is hiding in the grass lets loose. The fusillade of rifle fire cuts through the air. I stay close to the ground, adrenaline shooting through my veins, heightening my senses. I manage to swing my rifle up and rattle off a thirty-round magazine of suppressive fire.

Militiamen scramble, jumping out of their saddles, taking cover behind the hulking, muscled bodies of their horses. Katana snorts and paws the dirt. Another militiaman hits the ground.

"There's at least ten shooters out there!" Derek yells, his rifle in his hands. "We're dead if we move!"

"We have to reach cover!"

"There's no way to get there without being shot!"

I shake my head. That's not true. There's always a way. *Chris would find a way. Come on, Cassie. Think like Chris.*

I yank a white smoke grenade out of my kit.

"We need to cover our escape!" I shout. "I'll throw the first grenade, Derek will follow it with another, and then Uriah, Manny, Vera, Andrew and so on. We'll create a smokescreen!"

The rest of the militiamen are returning fire, shooting back at muzzle flashes in the moonlight. I don't hesitate. I pop the ring on the grenade and chuck it as far as I can into the open field. I jam my boot into the right stirrup of Katana's saddle and hang on for dear life to the restraints, keeping my body on one side of the horse. Uriah slaps Katana's rear flank and she charges forward. I've got one leg halfway over the saddle, using her body as a shield. I maintain a desperate grip as Katana leaps away. The grenades explode, billows of thick smoke curling into the air, creating a thick curtain across the field. More grenades detonate. More gunfire. Louder, faster, quicker.

Boom, boom, boom, boom!

Murderous rounds from a large caliber weapon hammers into action.

My arms burn, clutching the saddle as Katana sprints forward. Tears slide down my cheeks, an effect of wind and resistance and the torturous effort of maintaining a grip on Katana's saddle.

More grenades detonate. Men mount horses and follow me.

Bullets zip past, snapping the air with supersonic cracks, ricocheting off rocks and earth. I'm almost to the edge of the field – almost to the woods. My hands are sweaty, making it difficult to keep my grip on the saddle horn.

I grit my teeth and tough it out.

We reach the edge of the field. Katana stumbles just enough to throw my balance off. My grip slips and I hit the ground with a thud, rolling over and over in a tangle of arms and legs. The wind goes out of my lungs as two more grenades blast the field. I tumble into the bushes.

"Cover, cover, cover!! Come on!" Uriah yells.

Somehow, he has ended up next to me.

Figures.

I jump to my feet, unslinging my rifle, sighting muzzle flashes. Going through the motions of battle. After all, I am a sniper. This is what I do best. In a way, it is almost like being outside of myself – mechanically but expertly reacting to an attack with fluid, instinctive actions.

Mach and Katana are stamping the ground, stomping and snorting, rolling the whites of their eyes. Poor guys. I know the feeling. Firefights are no fun. Yet they don't run away. They stick with us. Amazing! They've been trained well.

The militiamen that have made it to cover stay concealed beneath bushes and behind trees, hitting the field with shots. I lie on my stomach, sweat and blood dripping down my forehead. I look through the optics of my rifle, searching the fields for shapes. There is nothing. Only muzzle flashes. I see one and snap a quick shot. A short yelp of pain follows.

"What are we dealing with here?" Uriah says. He has to shout to be heard above the sound of the gunshots and grenades. "Omega?"

"I don't think so!" I sweep the field once more with my scope. "This isn't their style."

More likely than not, we've run across rogue militia.

This could be *worse* than Omega. Rogue militiamen and vandals aren't organized into military units. They're made up of brutal gang remnants – without rules and regulations. Without a code of honor.

Not that *Omega* has a code of honor, but still.

You get my point.

A militiawoman – Sarah - is shot in the chest a few yards away from me. Her heart stops beating the second the bullet punctures her ribcage. She locks eyes with me for a split second, tossing a magazine in my direction. I crouch and roll, grabbing it. She is dead. I hold her final contribution to the fight in my hand, jamming it into my gun, reloading.

I shoot toward the enemy in the waving grass, returning fire methodically. Shoot three times, change my position, shoot one time, change my position...keep moving. Constant movement keeps me from becoming a target myself.

You're looking for the invisible enemy, Chris would say. *You're a sniper. You're one of the few people in this world that can find them. Look for irregularity. One element that's off.*

I settle and study the grass field through my scope again. There's a small patch of tall grass that has been smashed. By animals? By people? I don't know.

The grass is a clue, Chris whispers in my head. *It's telling you something.*

I sweep downward, at the bottom of the field. Just a few feet away from the smashed grass, there is a tiny – miniscule – black line in the dirt. I zero in on it. It's an irregularity. The one element that I'm searching for.

I carefully aim and squeeze the trigger. My shot is clean. It hits the line, and just as I thought, my optics picks up a spray of blood in the air. I move to the left and settle again.

"Aim low," I tell Uriah. "They're hiding in some kind of trench."

"Good eye, Cassidy!"

He spreads the word. I find only one more hostile target and I don't hesitate to take it out. Ten excruciatingly long minutes drag by. The horses are beside themselves with the noise from the gunfire. Then, suddenly, at minute eleven...it stops. There is no return fire from the trench, and I order my men to hold their fire. We don't want to waste ammunition.

The silence rings in a stark contrast to the noise we just experienced.

We stay hidden in the bushes. I struggle to maintain an even breathing pattern. I wipe the sweat out of my eyes.

"Alrighty, Commander," Manny huffs, breathing hard. "What's your take?"

I say, "Okay, I need three hunter-killers teams."

This is a tactic that Chris taught me. A Hunter-Killer team is usually composed of two men. Three teams equals six total assaulters. We will round the enemy from the left while someone stays here and holds down the main force. In other words, we're sneaking up on the enemy's flank while the rest of the militiamen attack them from the front. We'll box them in from two points.

"Derek, you take command while I take my teams," I say. "Keep their heads down so we can move. You'll hear us when we're in position. Got it?"

"Got it, boss. Go for it."

My three teams assemble around me – all of them veteran militiamen with common sense and great aim. We stay low in the bushes and trees, following the slight curve of the edge of the woods. It extends behind the grassy field. We move quickly and silently, too angry to be afraid.

I slip a little further along the wooded territory line, dropping down. I scan the field, searching for any enemy that might be lurking in the grass. It's clear. We're safe, and we're close to their position. Very close.

I see the ditch where they are hiding. They're idiots. Stupid tactics. There's nobody guarding their flanks. They're wide open to an attack. An *enfilade*, Chris would call it. I check the area one more time. All clear. My men see the opening, too.

"Okay, boys," I say, "Finish this."

In the next minute, we blow through ammunition in a vicious, overwhelming barrage of fire. There is screaming as the men in the ditch twist and fall, dead. Our bullets tear through their line of defense. I pop a red flare to signal Derek. He gives three blasts on his field whistle and his men stop firing.

"Skirmish line!" I yell.

I walk, reload, fire, reload and fire again. My teams spread out beside me, and together we finish off the rest of the enemy combatants in the ditch. They don't have a chance.

They are dead. All of them.

I choke on a shaky breath, gasping for air. Sweat sticks my uniform to my skin. I stop and look at the bloody carnage around me. I am horrified. How did I get to this place? How did this happen to me? How did I become such a killer?

My men are silent, checking their weapons, looking around them. I know what they're thinking. The same thing *I'm* thinking.

We have changed. All of us. We're not mere civilian survivors anymore.

"Good job," I say. "Now sweep through this and secure it. Do a search."

They stand around me, looking at me in a way that they've never looked at me before. Maybe they're just as horrified by what I'm doing as *I* am. Maybe I'm not the only one who doesn't recognize myself anymore.

I swallow a lump in my throat. "Move it," I mutter.

I turn away. I know that they can see the tears streaming down my face, but I don't care. If I didn't cry for this, I would be afraid that I'd lost all sense of humanity.

I slowly lower myself down, sliding on mud and grime. I crouch near the first dead figure. It's one of the men that I shot. There's a hole in the dead center of his head. I shudder, disgusted, and turn him onto his back. His entire body is clothed in black. His hands and fingers are wrapped in strips of black cloth. A black bandana is tied around his forehead. The only visible piece of flesh is the skin around his eyes – tiny slits on his facemask. I pull the facemask off. He's an average looking man. Maybe thirty years old. Uriah, Manny, Vera and Derek arrive at the scene, checking the perimeter.

In all, there are eighteen enemy ambushers.

"Who are these people?" Derek asks, kneeling next to me. "They're not Omega, and they're not militia."

"They're rogue," I shrug. "They probably wanted to steal our gear."

"Or they're mercenaries," Vera states.

I bite my lip. It's possible.

"Search their uniforms for any kind of identification," I say.

My dad used to call this *pocket litter*. Clues to someone's identification. I go through the dead man's pockets, unbutton his jacket and search the lining. Nothing. There aren't even clothing tags. Everything is clean. No clues whatsoever.

"I don't like this," Andrew murmurs. He's sitting on the edge of the ditch, staring at the militiamen searching the bodies. "People have lost their minds."

I take the gun off the dead man's shoulder and unbuckle his ammo belt. I remove the ammunition and weapons, sorting through the valuable items – and the items that we don't have room to carry.

"We can't find anything," Vera reports. "They're clean."

"What's the age demographic?" I ask.

"Twenties to mid-thirties. No women. They're all in good shape, too."

"You might be right. Mercenaries."

Andrew stands up. "Which means they were working for Omega," he says. "And when they don't report back, they'll send out a search party, find their dead bodies, and then they'll start tracking *us*."

"Then we should get moving," Manny suggests. "This isn't the most relaxing rest stop I've ever taken, anyway."

"We have to hide the bodies," Vera tells me. "They'll find them eventually, but if we make them search, that's extra time that we can buy ourselves to hit Los Angeles before Omega starts looking for us."

"Good plan," I approve. "Let's move."

The militiamen find a spot in the woods that could pass for a pit. With the manpower of twenty-five, the eighteen dead men are moved into the hole and covered with leaves and shrubbery. Under normal circumstances, I would suggest that we burn the bodies. Leaving them to rot in the woods is morbid – and I don't believe that it's humane, even if these people *were* trying to kill us. But we don't have the time. So we remove traces of our presence in the woods and backtrack to the ditch, clearing away brass and footprints. By the time we're finished with it, no one would be able to tell that there was a firefight here. Not unless they were looking really hard and they *knew* what to look for.

"Okay, we're good," I say. "Nice work, boys."

The words taste bitter in my mouth. Congratulating people for hiding dead bodies is *not* something I thought I'd be doing. Ever.

"The horses have been tended to," Manny announces as we walk towards the woods again, "but they're jumpy from the gunfire."

"They'll get used to it if they hang around us," I say.

"True story," Uriah comments.

"A little gunfire now and then builds character," Manny adds.

I laugh. It feels good, considering what a depressing night it's been.

"Shall we move on, my girl?" Manny asks.

"Yes," I reply.

I want to get as far away from here as possible.

Chapter Six

The next morning, exhausted, we stop and rest the horses again. I stroke Katana's nose, fighting tears. How many militiamen died last night? Three. Good men and women, volunteer soldiers just trying to do what's right and defend the things they believed in. They were under my command. I'm responsible for their deaths...aren't I?

I press my cheek against Katana's neck and stifle a sob.

I can't let anyone see me cry. Not now.

So I take a deep breath, blink back the tears, and try to force it out of my head. Someday, when this nightmare is over, I'll be able to stop and let the emotions roll in – if I'm not an emotional zombie by that point. But today is not that day.

Vera walks around the front of Katana and stands there in silence. I don't look at her.

"It wasn't your fault," she says suddenly. Harshly.

I stare at her. My eyes are red.

"It was," I reply. "They were my men."

She crosses her arms.

"We all volunteered for this, and we all know it's a suicide mission," she continues. "You're the one who keeps pointing that out. For the love of God, Cassidy, just do your job."

She exhales rapidly – as if she were holding her breath for the entire conversation – and stalks off. I blink a few times and smile. Bewildered? Yes. Confused about her intentions? Sure. But she has a point.

This *is* a suicide mission.

These militiamen and woman are here *voluntarily*.

If people die, it is not *entirely* my fault, is it? It's horrible, yes, but it's the price of war. The price of fighting for something you *really* believe in. The ultimate sacrifice.

The realization that I must carry their deaths as a burden for the rest of my life is harrowing. The price of leadership.

I close my eyes and scratch Katana behind her ear.

"We'll make it through this," I whisper.

She shakes her head, nickering. I laugh.

"You doing okay over here?" Manny asks. "I could have sworn you were talking to yourself."

"I was talking to the horse. Remember, I'm a horse whisperer."

"Ah, yes," he says. "A woman of many talents. I remember." He pauses and assesses Katana. "Your horse likes you."

"I get along well with animals."

"So I noticed. But what about people?"

"I can take them or leave them."

Manny's weathered, wrinkled face dissolves into an amused grin.

"I've often felt the same way, my girl," he says, "but in the end, it's not animals or trees or the universe we're fighting for. It's *people*."

"Yeah," I mutter.

"People aren't all that bad," he counters.

"I beg to differ. Omega is nothing but a bunch of people, and they *suck*."

He laughs.

"That, my girl, is the truth," he says. "We should talk more often. Your philosophy is entertaining."

"No more entertaining than *yours*."

"Oh, now I could debate that. The things that I've seen-"

"-Are probably things we never want to hear about," Uriah interrupts. His National Guard baseball cap is pulled low over his black hair. His left cheek is scraped up. He looks at me. It's an intense gaze – then again, when is it *not* with Uriah? "How far are we from the perimeter of the city?"

Manny answers, "Two days. Maybe three. Depends on if we get caught in any more firefights. Those always stretch the arrival time." He winks. "What I'm more worried about is Mad Monk Territory."

"Excuse me...*what?*" I demand.

"Didn't Arlene mention it to you?"

"I think I would remember that."

"It's in a fifteen mile stretch of territory before the city," he says. "A religious order of monks took over the area. They were driven out of the city by Omega, and since Omega doesn't take kindly to any religious groups of any kind...well, they're living in the mountains."

"Omega doesn't take kindly to *anything*," Uriah says. "Why do they call it Mad Monk Territory?"

"It might be because of the murders." Manny reaches in his back pocket, and pulls out his ever-faithful flask. I was beginning to think he'd lost it. "Dozens of survivors leaving Los Angeles have been found dead on the trails. They say it's because the monks went mad." He shrugs. "More likely than not, they're just a little bit...stir crazy."

"It doesn't sound like religious monks to me," I state, tracing the knife on my belt with my finger. "It sounds like a gang. Can we bypass the territory?"

"Not unless you want to add another week to our trip."

"Screw that," Uriah comments. "We need to get to L.A. *now*."

Manny pulls a map out of his saddlebag. He folds it in half and points to a stretch of mountainside about thirty miles outside of Los Angeles.

"This is Mad Monk Territory," he says. "Chances are, we'll be able to go straight through it and we won't have a problem. But...on the off chance that we *do* run into some crazies..." he lifts the map up. "We'll be in big trouble."

"We know how to handle trouble. Besides, we don't have a choice," I say. "Chris can only survive interrogation for so long. We've got a deadline to keep."

"If we want to get to the city in under a week we have to," Uriah agrees.

"Excuse me." Andrew has worked his way through the mass of horses and militiamen. His dark sunglasses are hiding his eyes. Three radios are strapped to his belt. Our radioman, ever exceptional and alert. "I've heard a lot of talk about the Mad Monks on the Underground radio over the last few days, and we do *not* want to run into these people."

"What have you heard, Andrew?" I ask.

"Civilian victims and Omega soldiers have been found in pieces," he answers. "Omega, militia, civilian. They're not showing any preference. They're just killing randomly."

"Why doesn't Omega just take them out?" Vera says.

"They don't have the time or the resources," I reply. "Besides, what would Omega want with miles of dry brush and grass? It's not their number one priority." I look at Andrew again. "What else do you know about them?"

"We don't know that they're really *monks*." He cracks a smile. "They dress the part. Robes and hoods and shaved heads, but other than that, all I know is that they like to kill things."

"Sounds like an urban cult," I remark. "There was a gang called the Metro Monks when I lived in Culver City. They were always a big problem for the Los Angeles Police Department. My dad used to talk about them a lot."

"It could be an offshoot of the same gang," Uriah suggests.

"It wouldn't surprise me. Even the criminals left Los Angeles when Omega came. They're locked outside, too."

I look between Manny, Uriah and Andrew.

"What do you guys think we should do?" I say.

I need all the advice I can get.

"I say we risk it," Uriah replies. "We're in this to get Chris Young back, and if we bypass the territory, this operation will take a week longer than we planned and he could be dead. That defeats the mission."

"But we can't accomplish the mission if *we're* dead," Vera adds, flat.

"That's a risk we'll have to take," Uriah answers.

"It's not like we couldn't take the Monks in a fight," Andrew adds. "We could. It's just the possibility of casualties. That weakens our chances of success."

"That's how we live our lives anymore," I point out. "We go through. Any objections?"

Silence. Good.

Mad Monk Territory, here we come.

Chapter Seven

"I don't get it," I told Chris. *"How come you know so much about me, but I don't know anything about you?"*

He settled against a tree. The memory is still clear, despite the fact that it happened nearly a year ago.

"Don't look at me," Chris said. *"You're the one who likes to figure things out."*

*"And you **don't**?"* I stopped to retie the laces on my boots. *"I just don't know a lot about you. I mean, I know where you come from and who your parents are...but I don't really know **you**."*

"What do you want to know, Cassie?" he chuckled.

"All of your dark secrets."

*"Ah, but those are **mine**."*

"One of these days..." I trailed off, watching the sunrise on the horizon. It was beautiful. One of the few moments of peace we'd had in weeks. *"I just want to know who you are,"* I muttered.

That's all I wanted.

It's all I still want. There are so many questions about Chris Young that have always been left unanswered. As a twenty-eight-year-old Navy SEAL, his world experience has always been far advanced in comparison to mine. What made him such a good leader?

I don't know. I don't have the answer to anything these days.

Mad Monk Territory isn't as scary as I thought it would be. The mountains are beautiful, rolling. Nothing here has been burned or decimated by Omega forces. Nature is still intact. We've been riding for hours, and I hate to admit that I'm *sore*. My hips, legs and lower back are strained from maintaining a position in Katana's saddle for such long periods at a time.

I'm not the only one who's feeling battered, either.

My militiamen are used to constant movement, hiking, climbing, and sneaking around. Sitting on a horse is a whole new ballgame. It hurts.

"We've got another full day before we hit Los Angeles," Uriah says. "I suggest that we camp for the night and travel the rest of the way tomorrow. The horses need to rest."

I keep my eyes on the trail, thinking.

"I don't think it's a good idea to camp in this area," I reply.

"There's been no sign of hostile activity yet."

"Exactly. *Yet*." I shake my head. "We'll scout for a good area to camp when we're out of here."

Uriah doesn't continue to press me, but I can tell that he disagrees. He's probably sore, too. But I don't want to be ambushed by psychos. That would put a serious cramp in my style. We've already had enough surprises on this mission, anyway. I'm not up for any more.

As night falls, we rest the horses, feed them, and give them water. We eat a small meal ourselves – enough to keep us moving – and mount up again. In the darkness, we have to move slower. We don't want our horses to trip on rocks or ledges. They're not invincible anymore than we are, and we have to keep a sharp eye out for them.

"Oh, my *God*!" Vera gasps. She pulls back on the reins of her horse, coming to a halt. "Up ahead!"

It's difficult to discern shapes and sounds in the darkness, but when I concentrate, I can see what she's looking at. Dozens of poles have been pounded into the ground up ahead. They're staked on top of a hill.

"What is it?" I breathe.

"People." Vera doesn't mince words. "Look harder."

I have keen eyesight, and the closer I look, the more I see. Dead bodies are tied to the poles. They're not very old, either. Clothing, hair and flesh are still intact.

"We need to get the hell out of here," Uriah says.

"No argument there," I reply.

I swallow a lump in my throat. Seeing dead bodies is nothing new to me at this point. But this isn't simple shock. This is sadism. We dig our heels into the sides of our horses and move away from the hill. My heart beats faster.

I don't want to die like that.

I have to live. I have to get to Chris...

And then something happens that I have never seen before. A silent bolt of light flies through the air and hits the side of the trail. The grass ignites, creating a tiny fire. Manny slaps his horse's side.

"Ride!" he yells.

More fiery bolts slice through the air. What are they? They're silent. They don't explode upon impact, either. I hunker down and hold on tight to Katana, shouting orders to my men.

That's when I realize that the bolts are *arrows*.

Mad Monks!

What is terrifying about this attack is that there is no noise. No yelling, no gunfire, no explosions, no vehicles. Nothing but the pounding of hooves against dirt and the occasional thud as a militiaman is knocked off his horse. Up ahead, Uriah is struck by a flaming arrow. He loses his balance and falls off Mach's back, slamming against the dirt. He tumbles a few feet and then drops again, rolling. His coat is on fire.

My militiamen whirl around on their horses and return to help the fallen militiamen. I raise my rifle to my shoulder and snapshot a few rounds into the grass, following the trail of the arrows.

Uriah continues to roll. He tears off the jacket and throws it to the ground, crawling closer to his horse – which has now taken off into the night, spooked.

I pull back on Katana's reins. I reach my hand out for Uriah. He grabs my wrist and swings himself behind me, gripping my waist. I spur Katana forward. We keep our bodies close to the saddle, trying to avoid making ourselves an easy target. But there is nowhere to go. There is nothing but open fields in every direction. No woods. No cover. And there are at least twenty figures emerging from the shadows. They're silent as cats – and so are their weapons.

This isn't the kind of warfare I'm used to.

"Whoa!" I scream, pulling Katana back. A group of men with bows drawn and silver arrowheads gleaming against the moonlight is blocking the trail up ahead. A ring of men is closing in around us. The horses rear up. Flaming arrows plunge through the sky, into the ground, forming a fiery ring around us. Uriah shouts, but I can't make out what he says over the sound of the horses whinnying and snorting.

The monks – or whatever they are – approach us. Uriah draws his handgun and the bows come up. I stay his hand.

"Don't," I say.

He slowly holsters the gun, wincing in pain.

The monks close in. They're wearing beaten clothing, long robes over combat fatigues and shirts. They carry bows. A quiver of arrows rests across their backs. I notice that they all sport the same shaved hairstyle. But they are not armed *only* with arrows. They've got guns, too.

"Do we run for it?" Vera hisses. Her horse is spinning around, rearing up. "Cassidy?"

No. Running for it would be…inadvisable.

Someone will be sacrificed in the process. I share a glance with Manny. He shakes his head. It's no good. We're boxed in. We've been trapped by the same techniques that we use on Omega.

"Who trespasses on this holy land?"

A particularly tall, dark-skinned monk yells at us. Two white, vertical streaks are painted under his eyes.

I shout, "Travelers! We're just passing through."

"What is your purpose?"

"We're going into the city!"

"The City of Angels?" The tall monk pulls his hood back, revealing a scarred face. "It is now nothing more than the City of Demons. This is the first I've heard of anyone attempting to get *into* the city."

"We have our reasons," Vera snaps.

The fire is still crackling around us. The monks stand their ground. But the horses have calmed down a bit, and I am resting on Katana's saddle, making eye contact with the tall monk.

"Are you Omega?" he asks.

"No."

"Are you thieves or vandals?"

"We're with the National Guard."

The tall monk regards me with a look of total skepticism.

"Are you in charge here?" he says.

"Yes." I look around the circle again, consciously checking to make sure all of my men are here. "Look, we're not here to fight with you. We just want to get to the city."

"What's in the city that's so important?"

I don't answer his question. Instead I say,

"We have business there."

He studies our uniforms.

"You're not dressed like mercenaries," he states.

"That's because we're *not*," I reply. "We're militia. We were with the National Guard, and we're on a special mission into Los Angeles. Please, just let us go."

The monk strokes his chin. He looks thoughtful.

"Your name?" he asks.

"I'm Commander Hart," I answer. "We're enemies of Omega, and if you are with them, you are our enemies, too."

His lips twitch.

"Father." A tall, thin Monk emerges from the circle of hooded men and approaches the man that I have been talking to. "This woman, she may be of the prophecy."

Vera's mouth drops. I give her a fierce warning look:

Say nothing. Let them be crazy.

"She is of the Guard, and she is traveling into the City of Demons," the thin man continues. He is staring at me with electric, nearly possessed eyes. "Am I wrong, Father?"

"You are not wrong," Father replies. A new emotion lights his features: curiosity? Amazement? I'm not sure. "And her hair...is flaming."

I self-consciously touch the ends of my curly red hair.

Yes. Flaming. Whatever.

"Tell me, Commander," Father says, "Do you go into the City of Demons to destroy the evil ones who infect our home?"

I blink. And then,

"Yes."

I don't even have to look at Vera to know that her mouth is still hanging open.

"If this is true, and you are of the prophecy, any enemies of Omega are friends of mine," he replies. "I am called Father Kareem, and these are my men. We are the Monks of the Order of the Arrow."

"What's with the robes and the flaming arrows?" Uriah demands, keeping one arm around my waist.

"We are the true monks," Father Kareem says calmly.

And apparently that's supposed to explain everything.

"How far are we from the city limits?"

"Not far," Father Kareem replies. "This is our territory, though. We can take you where you need to go, on the condition that you are discreet and pay proper homage to the Order."

He smiles slightly.

Father Kareem gestures to the horses. "These are magnificent beasts," he remarks.

I can't disagree with that.

"So. Father Kareem," Manny says, "can we get a move-on here? We're on a tight schedule. Lives hang in the balance."

If Father Kareem is annoyed with Manny's bluntness, he doesn't show it.

"Lives are always in the balance," he says.

"We need to get to Toluca Lake," I tell him. "Do you know the way?"

"I do." He gestures to his men. They lower their bows and arrows. "We'll be there by morning."

I close my eyes for a brief second and thank God.

The monks are not our enemies.

For now.

Chapter Eight

"So this is Los Angeles?"

We rein our horses and stop to overlook the sprawling urban landscape below. Uriah is not impressed. Neither am I, to be honest. The last time I looked across the skyline of the grand city of Los Angeles, the EMP had turned the city into pure chaos. Airplanes fell from the sky and flames lit the boulevards. Civilians roamed the streets in mobs, looting and vandalizing.

This is different.

This is dead.

In the early morning sunlight, the skyscrapers are little more than empty husks. Many of them are burned and falling apart. Others are riddled with gaping holes. Giant, pockmarked monuments to a fallen civilization. There is no noise. The sound of aircraft flying overhead is gone. Traffic helicopters are nowhere in sight.

The remains of the 405 freeway twist through the city. From our vantage point, the thousands of abandoned vehicles on the interstate look like a mass of dead insects. Everything is gray. Morbid.

Quiet.

"You've never been to L.A. before?" I say.

Uriah replies, "Never traveled much."

"Well," I sigh. "Los Angeles wasn't perfect...but it wasn't like this, either."

"This gives me the creeps," Vera mutters. "Where is everyone? I thought L.A. was an Omega hotspot."

"It is," Manny replies, popping his flask open. "This was a city of ten million people – most of them either dead or fled. Now it's an Omega base. They're just not making themselves real visible."

"Intelligence reports say that Omega troops are coming through the Port of Los Angeles, anyway," Andrew adds. "That's a few miles away. I don't think Omega has enough troops to send out more than random patrols."

"There's no steel ring around this city," Uriah remarks.

"We've brought you this far," Father Kareem says. "You can find your way from here."

I start, because I'd almost forgotten that the Mad Monks were still with us. In daylight, their clothes are bland. They blend in with the grass and shrubs along the mountains. I glance around, studying the men. The group is diverse, with ethnicities ranging from Indian to Korean. They almost seem like ghosts. Silent and stony. Unmoving. Father Kareem is the only one who has spoken to us since they walked us the three miles to the border of Toluca Lake.

"Thank you for your help," I say. "This shortcut saved us hours."

"Yes, it did." He raises an eyebrow. "Commander?"

"Yes?"

He pauses. Then, "Bring Commander Young back alive."

I stare at him. I'm not going to ask how he knows that we are here to rescue Chris. I'm not going to confirm or deny the information. I simply nod slowly, salute him, and watch as he silently returns to the hills. I watch *all* of them until they vanish from sight, reminding myself that yes – they were real. It wasn't some kind of weird dream.

"Where are we meeting our Underground contact?" Vera asks.

"About a mile," I say, pointing to portion of trees and burned houses in the distance.

"How far are we from Hollywood?" Andrew comments.

"Around seven miles, I think." I shrug. "I never used to spend time in Hollywood, except on weekends. Sometimes I'd visit the Boulevard with friends and see a movie."

Oh, those were the days.

And to think I used to complain about them.

"Lead the way, Manny," I say.

He nods, slipping the flask back into his duster, keeping it folded inside of his flight cap. I ease Katana down the trail and we dip behind the mountain again, out of sight. We could shave a few hours off of our journey if we cut right down the mountain, but that would leave us exposed to anyone watching the hills.

And after all of the trouble we've had, the last thing I want is attention.

We push forward. The closer we get to meeting our contact, the more nervous I become. The hills become smaller, and we enter into a residential area. Toluca Lake, according to our maps. The houses are gorgeous. Mansions. Much of the shrubbery here is either overgrown or dead. Most of the houses have been vandalized. Streaks of graffiti line rooftops and fence posts.

"Do we ride on the road or what?" Andrew asks.

"I guess we don't have a choice," I shrug.

We take the horses down the street; hooves clip clopping against the asphalt. It's a sound that probably hasn't been heard in Los Angeles for a hundred years. It's funny how things go full circle. You eliminate something from culture completely and then *bam*. Here it is again.

"This was super high end living," Vera comments. "Toluca Lake was a celebrity city."

"Yeah, I remember," I say. "I used to visit this place with my mom."

When I was a girl, we'd drive up and down every street, looking at the houses; pretending we were millionaires and that we could own any property we wanted. Come to think of it, it's one of the only happy memories I have of spending time with my mother.

"What are you smiling about?" Manny asks.

"Nothing," I whisper. "Just thinking."

He raises an eyebrow. But he says nothing.

As we continue, I tighten my grip on Katana's reins. The eerie silence of the neighborhood is creeping me out. The tension is thick in the air. At some point, something bad *has* to happen. It always does. I would be surprised if something *didn't* happen.

I'm not exactly a good karma magnet.

"Woodbridge," Manny announces. "We're here."

A faded, dark brown sign sits on the edge of an abandoned park. Trees and bushes are overgrown. The pond in the middle of the park – once beautiful and well maintained – has only a few inches of stagnant water remaining. Clouds of mosquitos hover over the surface.

"This used to be beautiful, too," I remark.

Coming here and seeing it like this...well, it's disturbing. I feel like I've fallen into the zombie apocalypse. We're stuck in a different dimension, but it's actually the sad reality.

"Stay on your horses," Manny warns. "If we've played this right – and I think we have – our contact should be on the other side. By the playground."

Vera mutters, "We come to Los Angeles and meet up with an Underground contact in front of *playground* equipment."

"If it bothers you so much, you can always go back to Fresno," Andrew snaps.

Vera looks surprised to hear him talk that way to her. Instead of coming up with a stinging retort, she shuts her mouth and sets her jaw. Silent mode.

Good. Silence is good.

And then I see him. He's sitting on the edge of a park bench on the right of the playground equipment. He's wrapped up in a black coat and scarf, watching us. Motionless. Behind him is a row of wrecked housing.

"Is that our man?" Uriah asks.

"I guess so," I say. "There's only one way to find out."

Manny leads the way.

I bring Katana to a halt and dismount. The grass is dead – it snaps under my boots. The man on the bench doesn't move. He stares at me, unmoving.

As I get closer, Katana hesitates. I catch a whiff of something. It's probably the stagnant pond – setting water smells disgusting.

"I'm Yankee One," I say, palms up. "And this is my team."

The man doesn't move. In fact, he doesn't even *blink*.

I step closer. His skin is pale. I sniff the air.

Oh, God. One eye is red and glassy, and I notice a purple bruise on the side of his face. He's dead.

"That is *disgusting*," Vera complains.

"So much for our contact," Uriah says. He dismounts his horse and studies the corpse. "He's been dead for a couple of days – no longer than that."

"Do you think Omega did this?" Vera wonders.

"No. Gangs, most likely," Manny replies. "If it were Omega, they would have questioned and tortured him before he died. This fellow looks like he was hit in the head once." Manny examines the dead man's head. "Yes. Blunt force trauma."

"Are you a doctor now, Manny?" Vera asks, blasé.

"As a matter of fact-"

"-We can take a trip down memory lane later," I interrupt. "Somebody left him here for a reason."

"So we could find him," Andrew states. "It's meant to scare us."

"Well…" I look around. "Are we scared?"

No one answers. I look around at my team, alert and in defensive formation, awaiting threats. Waiting for my word.

"I'm going to take that as a no," I surmise.

In truth, I'm quaking on the inside. Our contact is dead, which means we'll have to find somewhere to take the horses before we head into the city on foot. And anybody who is sadistic enough to leave a dead man sitting upright on a park bench *does* scare me.

I'm not entirely fearless.

"He was supposed to take us to the Way House," Vera says, tapping the dead man's shoe. "Now what do we do? What do we do with the horses?"

"Commander, on your six o'clock," Uriah says.

I turn quickly, noting the urgency in his voice. A man is standing on the edge of the park. His hands are up, showing that he is unarmed. My militia is already on him, surrounding him as quickly and efficiently as a pack of wolves.

The man is dressed in sandy combat fatigues and a leather jacket. His jet-black hair is shaggy and overgrown. I blink, recognition dawning on me.

"Oh, my God," I say. "Alexander Ramos."

———————————

I don't even think about what I do next. I cross the distance between Alexander and I. I throw my arms around his neck and give him a tight, relieved hug. He doesn't return the hug – but he doesn't shove me away, either. I take that as a fairly positive sign.

"How is this *possible*?" I whisper.

Alexander Ramos is supposed to be dead. Yet here he is, alive. "Ramos?" Derek grabs his hand. "What happened, man? What are you doing in Toluca Lake?"

"We thought you were *dead*," Vera states matter-of-factly.

"Technically, you *are*," Manny mutters.

"Long story," Alexander replies gruffly. He's purely non-emotional about the reunion. Unsurprising. He was never the touchy-feely type. But I can bet that if Sophia Rodriguez had known that we would find Alexander on this mission, she would have come with us.

"Are you supposed to be our Underground contact?" Andrew asks.

"I am," Alexander confirms.

"Who's the dead guy on the bench, then?"

"He *was* your contact." Alexander looks right at me. "He didn't come back to base, so they sent me out."

I exhale. Yet another man dies this day.

Suck it up, girl.

"We should get moving, then," I say. "We've had enough run-ins with gangs and mercenaries on the way here."

"Mount up," Alexander commands. "Cassidy, I'll ride with you."

I pull myself onto Katana's saddle. She snorts softly. He swings into the saddle behind me, keeping an arm around my waist. Six months ago I would have thought this was awkward. Now it's just standard procedure.

"Go that way," Alexander points, gesturing to a boulevard that shoots through a once prestigious neighborhood of mansions and apartment complexes. "We'll go about two miles before we hit the Way House."

I tap Katana's flanks with my boots and she trots forward. Considering the long journey she's been on – that *all* the horses have been on – she's holding up well. But she's tired.

"So are you going to tell us how you're still alive?" I ask. "Or are you going to keep it a secret?"

"It's a secret," he answers. "For now."

"Oh, come on, Ramos...we've had a long trip. At least give us a hint."

If he's smiling, I can't see it.

"Later," is all he says. But I do notice that he searches the platoon several times. He's looking for Sophia, I guess. And when he doesn't find her, he asks, "Where's Rodriguez?"

I answer, "She didn't come."

He doesn't seem to believe me. "She always comes," he says.

"Well...she didn't come this time."

"Why not?"

"She's dealing with issues."

"She's a basket case," Vera comments.

I shoot her a look. She shrugs.

"What happened that I don't know about?" Alexander asks.

I pause for a few moments. Then, "Jeff is dead."

"*What?*"

"And so is Max."

Alexander says nothing. After a few moments of heavy silence he says,

"And Commander Young…do we know for sure that he's alive?"

"No. But that's why we're here."

"It could be a fool's errand."

"It could be."

"Let me guess: the rescue unit was your idea."

A bittersweet smile tugs at the corners of my mouth.

"Yes," I say. "But they volunteered."

"And you're in charge?"

"I was elected."

He grumbles something that I can't hear.

"How's that working out for you?" he asks.

"It is what it is," I reply.

We ride about two miles up the road, coming to an oversized lot closed in with a stone security wall and thick shrubbery. It's impossible to see what's inside. The front gate rolls open as we approach.

Obviously somebody has been watching and waiting for us.

We take the horses inside, coming to a halt on a huge cobblestone driveway. A Spanish-style mansion is surrounded by bushes and trees. Soldiers are milling around the front yard. They approach us and take the reins of the horses. Alexander dismounts and I follow suit, keeping Katana with me.

"This is a Way House, huh?" I say. "Nice."

"It belonged to Jay Leno at one time, so I've been told," Alexander remarks. "But that's just a rumor." He pats Katana's flank. "Good horse."

"How many men did you start with, Cassidy?" he asks.

I look at my platoon, weathered and beaten by the stress of the journey.

"Thirty," I say.

"You've got twenty-six, now." He tilts his head. "Not bad, Hart."

I don't agree. Losing just a single person is losing one too many.

"It wasn't easy getting here," I state. "Between mercenaries and Mad Monk Territory, we're lucky."

"The Mad Monks are leftover remnants of mercenaries that betrayed Omega after the first attack on San Diego," Alexander says. "Surprisingly, they've become good allies of the militias."

"Wait. The attack on San Diego?" I reply. "Are you talking about the attack by *Mexico* on Omega?"

He nods. "Yes. A number of their forces...defected."

"Why?"

"Why do any men defect?"

"Because they're cowards," Vera interjects, folding her arms across her chest.

"Or because they know something that the leaders don't," I murmur. "Or they're in it for the money and the power. What do you know about Mexico, Alexander? Are they on our side?"

"There's a lot that's unclear right now. All we know is that Omega tried to push into Northern Mexico and Mexican forces pushed them right out. Clear into San Diego."

"Is San Diego out of Omega's hands?" I ask.

Alexander shakes his head. "I don't know," he replies. "Our radio hasn't been working. The last news we received was a week ago, and that was the message telling us that you would be headed this way."

Darn. It seems like everyone is in the dark about the Mexico question.

"These people will take care of the horses," Alexander says. "They'll be waiting for you when you come back."

I slowly pet Katana's nose. Her big, brown eyes study my face. "I'll see you again," I promise. "This isn't goodbye."

It feels like goodbye, though.

Someone takes her reins and leads her away from me.

"What now?" I ask.

"You come inside," he replies, "and we give you what you'll need to get Chris home."

A spark of hope ignites in my chest.

Remember why you're here, I remind myself. *Stay focused on the objective.*

I look up at the mansion.

Step one, completed. Beginning step two.

Chapter Nine

Harry Lydell.

I stare at a picture of his smug mug. Alexander is sitting on a stool in an empty dining room. A projector powered by backup generators is giving everyone a peek of what we're getting ourselves into. And for most of the people here, knowing our enemy is step one.

My rescue unit has been fed and cleaned up in the last couple of hours. Uriah was treated by certified medics. Thanks to the medication and equipment on hand here, he's no longer in pain from the bruising he took at the hands of the Mad Monks' initial ambush. The horses are being kept in a makeshift stable behind the house. Militiamen and women patrol the perimeter 24/7, and roving scouts constantly circle the area, keeping an eye out for unfriendly forces.

My team is sitting on the floor. I lean against the back wall, glaring daggers at Harry Lydell's image.

"Lydell is an Omega Prefect," Alexander says. "This basically makes him a General."

An award for selling the militia out to Omega.

"He oversees negotiations for Omega," he continues. "The parley between Lydell and Commander Young was one of many duties that he performs."

"Harry said he was working for someone named Commander Cho," I say.

"Cho is dead," Alexander answers. "He was killed. We learned this shortly before the radios stopped working."

"What's wrong with your radios?" Andrew asks.

"It's not a problem on our end. Omega's gone radio silent." Alexander stands up, pointing to Harry's face. "Lydell is also in charge of the Officer's Prison. It's a POW holding center for high-ranking militia officers. They're interrogated here, and most of them are eventually executed."

Executed?

"How long do they hold them there before they're executed?" I say. It's a question that I have to force myself to ask. "Days, weeks?"

"It depends on the importance of the prisoner." Alexander raises an eyebrow. "Chris is important."

That's all he says.

I take it as an implication that there's a chance that Chris is still alive.

"Why haven't you already tried a rescue mission?" I demand.

"We did try," Alexander states. "And we failed."

"Why?"

"We weren't able to penetrate the security system." Alexander's chest heaves as he takes a deep breath. "But we know the layout of the base now. It wasn't for nothing."

I fold my hands between my knees and take a deep, steadying breath. The projector flips to a new image. It's a photo of a squat concrete building. Cars and Humvees are parked out front as perimeter barriers. Armed men can be seen stationed on the roof.

"This is the POW Holding Center," Alexander explains.

"How did you get these photos?" Vera asks.

"We've got cameras that escaped the effects of the EMP," he replies. "The Holding Center is in downtown L.A. I'll give you the exact coordinates in a moment. What *you* need to remember-" he looks directly at me, "-is that security is going to be tight. This was a county jail before the war, a temporary holding center for prisoners being transported to court appearances. There are few weaknesses in the structure. No big windows to climb through. You'll have to go in hard and fast. You'll need the element of surprise."

"Sounds like a good time," Manny remarks.

"Sounds like suicide," Vera says.

"How many guards are we talking about?" I ask.

"Thirty to forty at the site," Alexander answers. "And you'll be downtown, which means the city itself will be thick with Omega. The civilian population that remains is submissive to Omega, so don't expect any help from them."

"Cowards," Uriah mutters.

"I think terrorized, enslaved individuals would be a more apt description," Manny replies.

"You have to get in and get out *fast*," Alexander presses, ignoring their negativity. "The Holding Center is near downtown L.A., so they've been landing helicopter and small aircraft at a base next door."

"We're walking into an Omega military base," Uriah states. "We're so dead."

"We're not dead *yet*," I counter. "This isn't harder than some of the other stuff we've done."

That's not necessarily true, but I'm trying to stay positive here. After everything we've been through – from surviving the ambush in Sanger to standing up against a million man Omega invasion force – I know that we're capable of pulling this rescue off. It's simply a matter of executing a good plan.

Go into a fight with the mindset of zero casualties, Chris would say. *That's not how I was trained, but it's how we have to treat the militias, because our troops are finite. We can't send in more troops when we run out. We've got to keep our guys* **alive***.*

That's the thing. I've already lost four men on this journey. From a purely professional standpoint, my mission to reach Los Angeles would be considered a major success. But from a militia mindset, every single man is important. Losing just *one* is too many.

"You'll be going into the city on foot," Alexander continues. "It's the fastest, most effective way to infiltrate the urban area. You'll be able to slip unnoticed past the patrols...probably."

"What about gangs?" Uriah asks.

"Where's there's Omega, there won't be gangs," Alexander replies. "Out here you'll find them, but not inside the city. Omega's got too much firepower."

"We know how Omega works," Uriah says. "I think we can get to the Holding Center and get inside. It's getting back *out* that concerns me."

Same here, I think.

"Any thoughts, Alexander?" I ask.

Sure, I'm the Commander. But I'm not above asking for help.

"I've got a few," he answers. And this time, he almost smiles.

Alexander Ramos was Chris's friend. There was a time when they were begrudging allies; I can remember when they did nothing but argue. But as the weeks and months of grueling militia life passed, they became more than commanding officer and soldier – they became *friends*.

Alexander went MIA on a scouting mission a couple of weeks ago before we lost Chris. It was difficult on everyone to lose such a respected soldier. It was hardest on Sophia Rodriguez – she loved Alexander.

If only she had come with us.

"I find it hard to believe that Sophia stayed behind," Alexander comments. We're standing in the kitchen of the mansion. I've got a cup of water in my hand. My fingers are shaking. I don't know why. Raw nerves and fatigue, I guess.

"So do I," I reply. "But she did."

"She's loyal to you, though."

"She's...hurt. She thought you were dead and then Jeff died." I take a sip. "After Chris went missing, she just got angry. Maybe she got tired of trying."

"Sophia has..." he trails off. "I may have underestimated you, Cassidy."

"I wish people would quit being surprised by me," I say.

"It's not a bad thing."

"It *could* be." I shake my head. "How did you end up here, Alexander? What happened?"

His face remains serious. He doesn't show a flicker of emotion.

"I wasn't wounded," he answers. "I was separated from my team. We were a few miles out and Omega mercenaries were working their way towards us. A few of my men were killed, others were wounded, and the rest of us scattered to stay alive. I ran out of ammo, then I got captured by Omega scouts." He folds his arms across his broad chest. "I was in a truck with a few other men. Halfway back to Los Angeles, the truck stopped and the guards pulled us out of the trucks. They interrogated and killed the prisoners in the truck, one by one, while I watched. Harry recognized my face. He wanted to keep me alive for questioning."

"How did you escape?" I ask.

"I got lucky." He exhales deeply. It's the first time I've ever seen Alexander Ramos look truly *sad*. "Omega got lax in security because I was the only prisoner in the truck. I had nothing to lose. They tied me up, but I managed to get free. The guard in the truck turned his back on me – his last mistake. When the truck slowed through a curve, I jumped out and ran. I ended up in Toluca Lake, the Underground picked me up, and now I'm here, running recon for them."

"Is this where you want to stay?" I press. "Or do you want to join the rescue unit? Or...do you want to go to Fresno with the National Guard?"

"I'd rather be with the *Mountain Rangers* in the hills," he replies. "But that's not going to happen."

"So what are you going to do?"

Such a long time goes by before he answers that I almost think he forgets that we're having a conversation. At last he says, "I'll come with you. And then I'll go back to Fresno with the National Guard."

A warm smile touches my lips.

I had a feeling that Alexander would find his way back to Sophia.

I was right.

"What are you going to do when the war is over?" I ask.

"Build a house. Leave the war behind me," Chris answers.

"Me too." I'm lying on my back, looking up at the sky. It is a warm summer afternoon. The newest recruits for the militia are training in the background. Chris and I have just returned from a successful reconnaissance mission.

"Cassidy?" Chris whispers.

I turn to look at him. His handsome face is troubled. He slowly takes my hand, studies each finger, then finally brings it to his lips in a soft kiss.

"Are we going to make it?" I ask.

Chris is the most positive, uplifting figure in the fight against Omega. But every once in a while, I see the vulnerability seep through. And I'm pretty sure I am the only one who is close enough to him to detect it. It worries me.

"We'll make it," he promises. "But it won't be without sacrifice."

"Maybe the United States military will step in," I suggest. "Maybe we won't have to do all of the fighting ourselves."

Chris smiles. It's a weary smile. He pulls me closer.

"We can't count on anyone but ourselves," he says.

"Is it really that bad?"

"Being on our own isn't a bad thing. Look at these people – they're inspired. They're fighting for something that they believe in." Chris hooks his arm around my waist. "It's made us stronger."

It always amazes me that Chris can pull something positive out of even the bleakest situation. I press an affectionate kiss against his lips. He grins – the first time he has seemed relaxed in days.

"I would do anything for you," I hear myself saying.

Does that sound desperate? I don't care. I mean it.

I still mean it.

After spending the night at the Underground base in Toluca Lake, I am well rested and ready to go. The militia stayed upstairs. Huge rooms have been stocked with mattresses, blankets and pillows. I stayed in a bedroom by myself at the end of a hall – the former master bedroom, I'm guessing.

When I wake up I find myself lost in a pile of expensive sheets and blankets. It's not even *close* to what I'm used to sleeping on: the dirt.

I roll out of bed. The room is dark. I light a lantern on the dresser in the corner; the room is huge, decorated with modern art. I sit on the floor and lace up my combat boots.

Come on, I think. *Wake up, Cassidy. It's time to go to work.*

I stand up. I pull my hair into a ponytail to keep it out of my face. I cinch up my belt, throw on my jacket and look myself over. Do I look like a battle-hardened commander? Or am I just a stupid kid from Culver City trying to play the part of a soldier?

Privately, I feel like a combination of both.

I grab my gear and open the door to the hallway. The militia is getting up, gathering their belongings. It's probably five-thirty. I find the stairs and enter the living room. Alexander is waiting, a grim expression on his face.

"Get a good night's sleep, Ramos?" I ask.

He grunts.

Yes. That's the Alexander I remember.

Uriah is standing silently in the shadow of the front door, tracing his finger down the length of a photo frame. His mood radiates depression. Under normal circumstances I would offer to cheer him up, but today I avoid him.

"All present and accounted for," Vera reports, descending the staircase. "Can we just get this over with?"

"Getting antsy, Vera?" I ask.

"I don't like sitting around here, doing nothing."

I don't disagree.

Manny suddenly barges in through the back door, tracking mud into the house. He looks wild and windblown – almost like he's been flying.

"What are you doing out there?" I ask.

"Checking on the horses," he replies. "They're settled in fine. Katana's comfortable." He jerks his thumb behind his shoulder. "The stable's just about as fancy as the inside of this mansion. Bloody horses are going to be spoiled rotten by the time we get back."

"They deserve a little pampering," I say.

"So do *I*," Manny answers.

I chuckle, stationing myself by the front door. The militiamen and women begin trickling downstairs, geared up and ready to go. Derek and Andrew are standing near each other, exchanging words in muffled voices.

"Well," I say, trying to keep the tremor out of my voice. "This is it. We've made it this far. We can make it the rest of the way."

There's a murmur of agreement.

"You have your orders," I continue. "We don't stop moving. If we play our cards right, we'll reach the prison today, and we can carry out our plan. Does anybody have any questions?"

Silence. There are a thousand questions to be asked, but in the end, only one thing matters: will we survive? I hope so. For Chris's sake. For the *militia's* sake. A lot is riding on this rescue mission.

To say nothing of the fact that if we *do* survive, we have to return to Fresno and face the wrath of Colonel Rivera.

"Let's go," I say quietly.

Solemnly.

Alexander opens the front door and we step outside together, into the pre-dawn. It's a dark October morning. *Zero-dark-thirty*, as Chris would say. It's cold, and it looks like the past week of fair, sunny weather is no more. The sky is cloudy. I smell rain.

"Commander?" Andrew says, falling into step with me.

We stand and wait as the gate rolls open. I stare at the empty street in front of us. Two expensive, abandoned cars are sitting on the side of the road. Leaves are piled in the gutters. The silence is like a physical weight on my chest. I feel overwhelmed with the forlorn atmosphere of this neighborhood – of this entire *city*.

"Commander," Andrew says again.

"Yes?"

"Are you okay?"

I raise an eyebrow. Then I lift one shoulder in a halfhearted shrug.

We move, locking and loading, rolling out in patrol formation, moving from cover to cover in the dull lighting of the early morning hours. Because of the caution we must proceed with, every city block seems to take hours to travel through. In reality, it only takes a few minutes. I'm acutely aware that every building could be hiding an enemy. We all are. Our rescue unit moves through the neighborhood with the silence and prowess of cats. Our presence here should go completely unnoticed – if all goes well.

By the time we reach the urban epicenter of Los Angeles, the classy, abandoned neighborhoods are no more. What remains is the part of Los Angeles that I was more familiar with as a child. The apartment complexes, the liquor stores crammed side by side with beauty parlors and pawnshops. Before the apocalypse, this was a bad area. It's almost improved with anarchy. There's not a soul in sight.

There is graffiti on the walls. Shapes and symbols in bright colors. *Semper Fi* is painted in yellow letters across a billboard for men's cologne. Weeds are growing through the cracks in the pavement, twisting around rusty cars and dead streetlights.

"Red light," Uriah mutters, standing at an intersection. The stoplights are bent, hanging at odd angles. A pile of rubble sits in the middle of the street. The back half of a strip of stores has been blown open. By the looks of it, it happened quite a while ago, too.

Wait a second.

I take a few steps closer to the back of the buildings. A deep crater is there. Black, charred, ashy soot is smeared along the remains of the structures. And in the center of the crater is a passenger jet. Or what's *left* of it. It's huge. The cabin alone spans the length of five shops. It looks like something exploded inside, causing the ceiling to rupture. The plane is sitting in two halves – as if it split right down the middle.

"This is one of the planes that went down the night the EMP hit," I breathe. "I heard them go down. I *saw* the first one."

"Nobody walked away from this," Vera remarks. "They died on impact."

"How many planes went down that night, do you think?" Uriah asks.

"However many got the brunt of the EMP's attack," I answer. "Some planes are protected from that kind of thing, and a lot of them were probably fine. But not all of them. Not *enough*."

What a horrible way to die. Hurtling to your death in a metal box, in a room full of strangers. None of the people that died here would even know *why* they were going to die. They probably thought it was a bomb or a freak accident.

How many children were on this plane?

I shudder.

"We should keep moving," I say. "It's not safe to stop."

I pull away from the decimated passenger jet, silently mourning the innocent civilians that died here. Everything within the city block has been totaled – destroyed by the explosion of the crashing plane.

I could have easily been caught in one of those explosions that night.

But I wasn't. Why did so many people survive – and why did others die? Why did mothers and infants and children have to lose their lives? They were innocent. Why did Omega's takeover require so much bloodshed?

It's an impossible question to answer.

We find two more passenger jets within the next hour. All of them were either landing or taking off from the Los Angeles International Airport – or LAX, as it's more commonly called.

Or *was* called.

I wonder if my mother survived the EMP? I think.

Since Omega's invasion, I have often wondered if my mother is alive. Where was she when the EMP hit? Did she leave the city? Did she escape Los Angeles before Omega attacked it with a chemical weapon?

Despite the fact that I was never close with my mother, it bothers me that I will never know what happened to her. And I guess that puts me in the same boat as millions of other people. People that have no idea what happened to their family members and friends.

Through everything, my focus was on two things: survival and finding my father. Once I found my father, survival was *still* my main focus. It still is, I guess. Only now I'm surviving for a *reason.* Surviving to fight Omega another day.

"Here's what worries *me,*" Uriah says in a low voice, falling into step with me. "If Los Angeles was attacked by a chemical weapon, are we breathing poison right *now?*"

"Unlikely," Andrew answers, overhearing us. "I'm betting that Omega used Sarin. We'll be safe to walk through the city without dying of radiation poisoning."

"What's Sarin?" I ask.

"It's an odorless, deadly poison," Andrew replies. "Before the EMP, there was a lot of it being used in the war in the

Middle East. It's a popular way to attack people without firing a shot."

"How long does Sarin last?" I say. "The effects, I mean?"

"On the body? It doesn't take more than a teaspoon to kill you." He shrugs. "It doesn't really linger in the air, though. We'd be dead already if it were still here."

"Good to know," Uriah says. "We could be breathing in poisoned air."

"That's the chance you have to take, coming back into Los Angeles," Andrew points out. "Besides, if Omega has set up headquarters here, it's *got* to be safe."

Good point.

Then again, Omega might know something that we don't.

As we burrow into the heart of the city, I see signs of Omega's presence. Posters and billboards have been covered over with the Omega symbol: the white O containing the continents of the world. One poster is taped to the inside of an abandoned storefront window:

UNITE

OMEGA REQUIRES ALL CITIZENS TO REGISTER FOR THE CENSUS

REPORT TO GENERAL HEADQUARTERS

COMPLIANCE IS MANDATORY

Uriah says, "What's that supposed to mean?"

"It means that registering for the census is a command, not a suggestion," Vera answers. "Anybody left alive in this city is probably registering. There's no such thing as flying under the radar once you give them your information."

"If they don't *already* have it," Andrew says. "Omega could probably pull up information on every citizen in the state based on Facebook pages alone."

"But the EMP wiped out the computers," Uriah replies.

"It didn't wipe out *everything*," Andrew counters. "Remember, Omega's got satellites and televisions and access to the digital cloud. The EMP was directed to wipe out *our* access to technology – not theirs."

"So you're saying my Facebook page is still accessible to Omega?" Uriah says.

"You had a Facebook page?" I remark, grinning. "What was your relationship status?"

He grimaces.

"Probably 'it's complicated,'" Andrew snickers.

Uriah whacks the back of Andrew's shoulder, and I laugh for the first time in hours. But when you really stop to think about it, there's a massive pool of information on the Internet that Omega could use to pull up information on anyone they want. That's how they found out where my dad used to work. That's how they knew Chris was a Navy SEAL.

The Internet. A scary place in more ways than one.

"I don't know what book face is all about," Manny comments," but I never had one. And I'm glad I didn't. Omega won't be able to find anything on me."

"They'll be able to find something," Andrew answers, "if they really want to." He pauses. "And it's *Face*book, not book face."

"Facebook, book face," Manny rolls his eyes. "Same thing."

"Citizens that are enrolled in the census," Andrew continues, turning to me, "have to report weekly to General Headquarters. They only get a certain amount of buying power in the stores, and they're given mandatory Omega jobs. Otherwise known as slave labor."

"How do you know this?" I ask.

"I listen to the Underground radio."

"It sounds like Omega's turned L.A. into a dystopian society."

"Dystopian? No. It's blatantly obvious that things are controlled by Omega," he says. "They're not trying to hide it. There's no illusion. The *question* is, who's really in charge?"

"So nobody can buy or sell without Omega approval?" Vera asks.

"You've got to have a registered Omega identification card to buy or sell *anything*," he explains. "And even then you can only buy a certain amount. I don't know what people are using for currency. The dollar is worthless."

"They're probably selling their souls, for all we know," Vera says.

During the fourth hour of our journey through the city, we change our route. The signs of Omega's presence are very strong here, and as we progress, I hear something in the distance. Voices? Machines?

We move through an alley. I stop, eyeing a fire escape at the back of an apartment complex. "I'm going to take a quick look," I say. "Stay here and keep an eye out."

"I'll come with you," Uriah volunteers.

Of course.

I curl my fingers around the rusty rungs of the ladder and climb. The building is only four stories. I reach the top and roll onto the roof. I can see clearly in all directions from here. Miles of buildings wind across the landscape in every direction. I can almost see the ocean from here.

Almost.

Less than three miles away, the signature circular skyscraper of Los Angeles towers above the ground. The windows over the top half of the building have been painted red. The white Omega O is visible in the center.

"I think we found General Headquarters," I say, sick.

"That's the beehive," Uriah replies. "Wow. They didn't waste any time making L.A. their home, did they?"

I shake my head.

Uriah remains silent for a few moments. Then, "Listen, Cassidy...about the kiss. I shouldn't have done that."

"You're right. You shouldn't have." I maintain my crouched position on the roof. In the distance, there is movement. Lots of movement. People? Probably.

Uriah swallows, resting his fists against his knees.

"I just...I care about you, Cassidy," he continues.

I glance at his face, hesitating. His expression is one of hope.

"I know," I reply.

And that's all I say. What else am I supposed to do?

I don't want to lead him on. I *won't*.

I jump over the ledge and climb back down the fire escape.

"Well?" Manny asks.

"There's people," I say. "A lot of them."

"All survivors," Andrew tells us. "But we can bypass them to get to the Holding Center. I think."

"You *think*?" Vera snaps. "You'd better be sure. We can't risk running into any more gangs."

"Hey, I'm just going by Underground intelligence," Andrew fires back. "It's not my fault if we walk into a firefight."

"It's nobody's fault," I interrupt, silencing them with a look. "We're going to stick to the plan and keep to this route until we get to the Holding Center."

It takes every ounce of self-control in my body to maintain a leader-like glare. To avoid dropping my gaze. I hold eye contact with Vera until she turns away.

We move around the back of the apartment building, walking down another alley. Garbage and human feces are piled in the gutters. The smell is horrific. We tie scarves around our faces to avoid being overwhelmed with the stench. I stop dead in my tracks, staring at two small human shapes crouched near the gutter. A little girl and what looks like her younger brother is pawing through the debris in the streets. Their clothes are nothing more than torn rags, skin smudged with dirt and grime.

They freeze, watching us with wide eyes.

"Oh, my God," Vera whispers.

"We should help them," Uriah says.

"No," I reply. "We can't."

"But Commander-"

"-No."

He makes a move to walk toward the children, then thinks better of it. He remains where he is, and we start moving again. The children are still motionless as we pass – almost as if they believe that if they stay still, they won't be seen. It breaks my heart. Children are starving in the streets, digging through garbage and human waste to survive.

This is what Omega has done to us.

It's just as devastatingly sad as it is infuriating.

"This is third world status," Uriah grumbles. "Why did this have to happen?"

"Because we're all human," I sigh. "And human nature sometimes screws everybody over."

"They were just children, Cassidy."

"I know." I pat his shoulder. "I didn't say it was right. It just *is*."

And what I don't say out loud is that we – as militiamen – are fighting to restore not just humane living conditions, but freedom. We're already doing our part – and more besides.

As we continue through the city, the image of the starving children haunts my mind. I try to push it away, focusing on my objective:

Chris. We're here to rescue Chris.

But the further we push, the more afraid I become. Streets and buildings that I was familiar with as a child have been destroyed. A clothing boutique where I bought my first pair of skinny jeans as a fourteen-year-old has been looted, covered with bright, vulgar graffiti. A bakery where I used to meet with my math tutor has been burned out. The faded sign

127

advertising discount scones and cups of coffee is riddled with bullet holes.

"Anarchy is hell," Andrew remarks. "Omega didn't do all this. *Citizens* did this."

"My dad said it was insane," I reply. "It took him three days to get out of here after the EMP hit."

"Was he on foot?"

"Yeah."

He's silent for a second. Then, "I was in Fresno. When the EMP hit."

"What were you doing?" I ask.

"Watching a movie." He laughs softly. "Me and my friends. We were at the theater, and all of the sudden the power just goes *out*. Nobody's phones are working, nobody's flashlights are working. The ushers are falling over themselves to get us out of there, and by the time we get home...my family's not even there. They're just *gone*." He closes his eyes. "I have no idea what happened to them. They just disappeared. The cars were still in the driveway."

"I'm sorry," I say, quivering. "What do you think happened?"

"I don't know." A pained expression crosses his face. "That's the worst part, I guess. Not knowing." He stops. "But maybe it's a good thing, too."

Yes. Maybe.

Sometimes it's better to be blissfully ignorant of the fate of the people we love, than to know what horrific fate they had to suffer. Or you end up like me, with memories of friends like Jeff Young getting shot on the battlefield.

I shiver.

No more of that.

Vera snorts, "I can't wait to get out of this Godforsaken place."

"We're almost there," I whisper. "Almost."

We can't be more than three miles away from the prison, and that knowledge makes my hair stand on end. Once we actually *reach* the prison, we have to do a quick recon, find a point of entry, infiltrate it, find Chris, get out and survive – all in the timespan of one day. It's a daunting task, but come hell or high water, I'm here to save Chris.

And I will not fail.

Chapter Ten

The Holding Center.

It looks exactly like the picture Alexander showed us. It sits on the corner of a boulevard in downtown Los Angeles. It's a basic jail structure, but an Omega symbol is now painted above the doorway, and the street rumbles with activity. Omega trucks are parked outside. Patrols make their rounds through the area.

A small aircraft base is stationed a block away from the Holding Center. It's an open area of asphalt and cement. The three warehouses in the back were previously marked with a storage company's insignia. It has now been replaced with an Omega symbol. Omega has cleared the entire area to make a runway and landing strip. I can clearly see two black helicopters from here.

We are crouched on top of a five-story building two blocks away, studying the layout. Alexander is on my right, Andrew is on my left. Uriah, Derek and Vera are silent as we scope out our surroundings. The techies – three people, including Andrew – review the coordinates and blueprints of the building for the hundredth time.

"Distraction, not destruction," Manny says in a low voice. "That's the name of this game."

"It might *turn* into destruction if we screw up," Vera replies.

"We won't," I say with confidence that I don't feel.

My heart is beating wildly in my chest. *Chris* is inside the building just two blocks away! He's so close...yet so far. I take a deep, steadying, calming breath and close my eyes. The fact that we have made it this far without dying is a testament to the fact that A) we're a highly skilled militia rescue unit or B) we're just lucky.

"So," Vera says. She looks at me. "The plan, Commander?"

A faint breeze rustles my hair. I shove my bangs out of my eyes as silence falls over the group.

You know the plan, make it work, Chris's voice whispers.

"Okay," I say. "Here we are. We're alive and we're still *very* capable of kicking Omega's butt. We'll have to use a little finesse, though. Distraction, not destruction, like Manny says." I stare at the Holding Center. "Thanks to Alexander, we know where the patrols are and around how many guards will be inside. Our advantage is that we're small, fast, and know how to hit hard. If we create enough confusion, Omega won't know what hit them. Our *dis*advantage is that we don't know where Commander Young will be. He could be anywhere in the building, with any of the POWs. Finding him will be time consuming, and that's where the element of distraction comes in handy."

"A few of you will keep the guards busy at the front of the building," I continue. "While the rest of us will infiltrate the building from the rear entrance. It's the easiest place to penetrate."

"I love being the distraction," Derek comments, smiling dryly.

"Yeah, you do," Andrew replies, smiling a little. "You're going to use every trick up your sleeve to keep them at the front of the building. We may not know *exactly* where Chris is, but we *do* know that the prisoners are in the back of the building, in the cells. That means we need to keep the guards away from that area."

"I'm planning on it," Derek mutters. "Where will you be, Andrew?"

"With me," I say.

"Alexander?"

"He'll be with me, too," I tell him. "Alexander knows the layout of the building best." I pause. "Derek and his team will meet up with us at a rendezvous point once they're done with their part of the mission. There will be too much chaos to try to hook up in the middle of the fight."

The cold heat of adrenaline burns my gut. An all-too familiar feeling.

Will I ever get used to this sort of thing?

"I'd guess we have about twenty minutes," I say. This is something that we already know, but I don't want anybody to forget that we're on a tight schedule. There is no room for mistakes. Not here.

"We can keep them busy and distracted for a long time," Derek replies, looking at me, "but that's only as long as they don't bring in backup."

"Which is why we'll only have about twenty minutes," I say. "If we can keep this isolated, we'll be good to go."

Despite the adrenaline rushing through my body, I feel steady – calm, almost. A controlled, directed anger. It's a brand new feeling. And I like it.

"And if we can't find Chris in twenty minutes?" Uriah asks.

It's the unspoken question, and now it hangs heavy in the air.

"Then we'll free who we can and get out," I reply firmly. "And we'll think of another way."

In my heart, I know that if we fail, there won't *be* another way. Omega will expect a second rescue attempt, and they will be waiting for us to try something. Harry Lydell would kill Chris. It would mean game over.

This is something that everyone *knows*, but nobody wants to say it.

There's no reason to.

"We'll wait until it gets dark," I continue. "Remember, in and out. Make it quick. Improvise, adapt and overcome. I don't want any friendly casualties. Understood?"

"Understood," Uriah echoes.

"Good."

I look around at the many faces watching me. All of them, good men and women – even the ones I don't necessarily get along with on a personal level. They're risking their lives for Chris – and for our cause.

"Vera," I say. "I want you with me."

She doesn't reply. She simply nods, her expression a perfect poker face.

Life is short. It's even shorter when you're a soldier. Do the right thing, because tomorrow, you might not get the chance.

The alley behind the Holding Center is big enough for prisoner transport trucks and buses. Steam rises off the damp, rocky asphalt. An Omega transport truck is parked near the rear entrance – a rollup metal door, ten feet tall. It's secure, so prisoners can't merely jump out of the truck once the door opens and run away. The sound of muffled voices and shouted orders echo off the walls of the buildings.

We wait. More than anything, I want to jump up, force my way inside the building and get this over with. But doing that would be suicidal. If we don't stick to the plan, we'll all die – and that would suck. Big time.

"How much longer?" Vera hisses.

"It's getting dark. Be patient," I reply.

Manny is picking at his shirtsleeve, preoccupied with a loose thread on the cuff. He looks relaxed, as always. I envy his ability to shut the stress out. The ability to simply *be*.

"You know," Manny whispers, "if we get away with this, it may be the first time Los Angeles has ever had a successful downtown jailbreak."

"So we're making history," Uriah says.

"Glorious history." Manny grins. "The best kind, of course."

In the stagnant white noise of the back alley – the hum of the Holding Center's generator, the echo of Omega voices – a detonation interrupts the rhythm of sound. The ground shakes a little. It's so familiar that I hardly blink.

"That's our cue," I announce.

A red security light begins blinking in the back of the building. The rear entrance rumbles upward a few beats later and fifteen black-clad Omega troops pour into the alley. All young. All men. All very foreign.

Each of my team members has an assigned sector – a specific job, a specific point of focus. I am completely shocked that fifteen troopers have flooded out of the building – I hadn't expected this much luck.

Nevertheless, my heart twists in my chest as I bring my rifle up to my shoulder and train my sights on one of the fifteen troops. Vera, Manny, Uriah, Alexander and myself each pull the trigger on our weapons. A sporadic smattering of rifle fire fills the air, echoing off the alley walls. Troops collapse at odd angles, dead before they even hit the ground. It's eerie. Our aim is so perfect that there is no screaming. Just fifteen gunshots and fifteen dead patrols on the asphalt, pooling in blood.

"Go, go, go!" I yell.

This is our chance. The rear entrance is *open*. We were not expecting this – I was expecting that we would have to blow it open.

Thwap!

A bullet whizzes by my head. I jerk to the side and roll into a crouch. A guard is standing in the open doorway, frantically making an effort to close the entrance. Uriah takes him down.

The dead trooper hits the ground with a thud. We push inside the door. And we move on toward the objective.

Good job, Derek! I think.

We stack and go, clearing the hallway corners and taking out moving targets.

It's cold and stale. Yelling and gunfire can be heard within the concrete confines of the building. The epicenter of the noise isn't too far away, either. Just at the front of the building, where Derek and his team are creating a distraction.

"Right, right, right!" I say.

This floor is empty. We veer down a wide hallway. Two Omega guards are fumbling in the corner for their weapons, probably left behind to guard the back of the building. My team is deadly. Vera and Uriah kill them instantly with controlled rifle fire.

Perfect.

This hallway is filled with cells. It's a standard county jail, with cement flooring and metal bars. The stench of vomit is powerful. We spread into the area, breathing hard, sweating. Check left, check right, scan for threats and the objective – Chris. The first cell holds a skinny man, the second cell holds a woman covered in hundreds of lacerations. My brain registers the fact that this is a torture chamber, but I have no time to dwell on it. We are moving too quickly.

In all, there are ten cells – all of them hold prisoners that I do not recognize.

"Bingo!" Uriah yells. There is a main switch at the end of the hallway – a literal emergency door release in case of fire. I slam my fist against it and the cell doors unclick. They are unlocked. The prisoners seem dazed at first – unable to believe that their cells have been opened.

I don't have time to make a speech.

"Keep going!" I shout. "Move it!"

Panic hasn't seized me...yet. I was expecting to find Chris here, on the first floor. I don't recognize any faces. None. Is he dead? Did Harry Lydell already order his execution?

Alexander grabs my arm and says, "This isn't *everybody*."

I nod and move swiftly to the stairs.

A lone guard is coming around the corner. I catch the movement of his body out of the corner of my eye. A symphony of keys jingle on his belt. I automatically shoot him in the chest, never hesitating for a moment. He hits the ground with a thud, a strangled scream still in his throat.

I drop to my knees and yank the keys from his belt.

We run through the hallway, taking another corridor that dives to the left. This one is longer than the others, and more heavily guarded. We quickly kill six more guards, and as the Omega casualties pile up, the timer in my head starts ticking faster. The more security we encounter, the longer it takes to reach our objective, and we've got just minutes to hit, rescue and run.

I spot something on the wall, above a door.

"Whoa, look up!" I say, skidding to a halt.

It reads: DIVISION FIVE

A cellblock we haven't searched yet.

I share a glance with Manny.

We go inside.

The hallway here is short with fifteen compact cells. Each one is nothing more than a door with a small slit for a window.

"Chris!" I shout. "Where are you?"

I pull back the metal sheet on the window and peek inside the first cell. An emaciated figure is sitting in the corner. A woman. An officer.

I toss the keys to Uriah.

I say, "Get them out." Then, "Chris Young! Are you here?"

Uriah discards the keys that he took from the guard in the hallway and finds the main switch to the cell doors – they open, just like they did on the floor below. The prisoners inside the cells are starved, beaten, and bruised. Many of them are covered in scabs and dried blood. The living conditions remind me of the Omega slave labor camp I was imprisoned in.

I come to the last cell. The man in the corner has long hair and a lean build. My mouth goes dry.

"Chris?" I say.

He looks up, but it's not Chris. Someone else. I have a borderline heart attack.

"He's not here," I state, numb. "Chris isn't here."

"He's here *somewhere*," Uriah replies, shaking me. "Don't give up."

God, please. Give me a break! I'm begging you!

Injured and weakened officers stumble into the hallway, disoriented and confused.

"We're Americans!" I say simply. "We're here to get you out." Then, "Do any of you know where Commander Chris Young is?"

I might as well ask. Seriously. What have I got to lose at this point?

My question goes unanswered. So I ask again, louder. This time, someone speaks up. It's the prisoner that I thought was Chris.

"He's upstairs," he croaks. His voice is broken by exhaustion. "I don't know if he's coming back or not."

A stone drops to the pit of my stomach.

"Stick to the plan," I tell Uriah. "We go upstairs."

Half a dozen officers manage to drag themselves into the hall with the help of my men. "Okay," I say, "stick with me. Officers?" I turn to the newly freed prisoners. "Run like hell and don't stop until you're safe."

The clock is ticking. Omega is now totally aware of our presence *inside* the building, and I'm guessing that we have seconds to locate Chris and get out of here before backup rolls in.

The prisoners separate from my team. We leave the hallway and head for the stairwell. We have studied the blueprints for this building so many times that I feel like I'm reenacting some sort of memory.

Manny and Uriah open an exit door and we enter the stairway. The metal steps echo as we stay in formation, climbing to the next level. Emergency sirens screech through the chamber.

We enter the stairway. Omega guards and officers are frantically crawling all over the office cubicles. Computers with lit monitors are sitting on every desk.

Computers. *Working* computers.

An Omega guard fires off a round and hits Manny in the shoulder. He drops to one knee and brings his pistol up, firing back. The soldier is slammed backwards in a spray of blood.

"This is an office area!" Uriah shouts. "Where's Chris supposed to be?"

"With Harry," I say.

I don't know how I know this – I just *do*.

I looked at the layout of the Holding Center more than anybody else. Harry Lydell's office is here – and if Chris is still alive, that is where he must be.

"Manny, are you okay?" I ask, breathless. I help him to his feet. He clutches his shoulder as blood gushes out of the wound. "Oh, my God. Uriah?"

"I've got it," he says.

Manny looks pale, and he is wincing in pain.

"Keep going," he warns. "I'll be right behind you."

"We're not leaving you," I state.

Tick tock, tick tock.

Bam, bam, bam, bam.

Fire and return fire. Gunpowder and smoke and screaming sirens. And I see Harry's office. Two big doors in the back of the room. I recognize them instantly from the layout plans I studied. A jolt of adrenaline seizes me. This is our last chance. We've barely got any time left.

"Just *go!*" Manny yells, sweat dripping down his face.

In that moment I know that I have to make a hard decision: save Manny or save the team? I swallow the horror of that realization. He slowly nods his head. He is down.

"We'll be back for you," I promise.

It's a false promise. We are out of time.

We move across the office, systematically coordinating our movements like a SWAT team on a raid. Our presence here is *definitely* not a secret anymore. By the time we reach the office doors, every single Omega trooper that stood in our way is either down or dead. We are just *that* efficient.

"Duck!" Uriah shouts.

I don't hesitate. I just do as he says. He fires a round over my head and a trooper falls dead, half of his body concealed behind the corner of a hallway. Well hidden. Almost the death of me.

"Thanks," I say.

He nods.

The office doors are marked with simple bronze plates that read:

DISTRICT PREFECT: HARRY LYDELL

The doors are locked and the wood is too heavy to break.

Tick tock...

"Come on, hurry up!" I command. "We're running out of time!"

Andrew straps a strip charge to the door and we take cover behind some metal filing cabinets. Five, four, three, two, one...*Boom!* The explosion shatters the door, sending splinters of wood everywhere.

I approach the door. I want to be the first one through. We push the doors aside and walk into the office. Desk, chairs, and a window overlooking the street below. Omega soldiers are rallying around the front of the building, returning fire, blindly attacking distant muzzle flashes. Smoke is rising around the building, a flood of gray fog on the Los Angeles avenue that has become a battlefield.

Brilliant, Derek, I think proudly. *Keep it up.*

But the office is empty, and my heart sinks again. Harry is nowhere to be found. Uriah walks around the desk and pulls open the drawers. He stuffs his pack with papers and maps. I just stand there, frozen for a moment. Disappointed. The hope drains out of me.

If Chris isn't in this building, then he's not alive.

It's as simple as that.

Panic seizes me. I fight to keep my breathing even, to maintain a grip on my nerves. I can't have a breakdown in the middle of a rescue operation. These men are counting on me to get them out of here alive.

"Manny, is there anywhere else we can look?" I ask, looking back toward the wall where we last left Manny.

No answer.

"Manny?"

Uriah gives me a confused look, Andrew searches the room.

"He's not here," he states. "What the hell?"

"He was *just* here!"

"He couldn't just disappear."

"He just did!"

Bam!

A gunshot ricochets off the wall. Bullets crack past my body. We drop down, instantly covering ourselves. Manny is nowhere in sight, and the alarm bells are ringing in my head. Four guards are moving toward us in the office, taking cover behind desks and cubicles. I fire a round at one and hit him square in the chest. He goes down. I roll backward and slide behind Harry's desk. My ears are ringing and sweat is pouring down my forehead.

"What happened to Manny?" I shout.

"He was here two seconds ago!" Uriah replies.

One shot, two shots, three shots...

What do I do? We have to go. We can't stay. This was the plan – get in and get out. If we can't find Chris, we have to leave. *Now.*

"We're done here!" I yell. "We've got to go!"

"But we haven't found-"

"-I *know*!" I hold my stomach, gasping for breath. "Believe me. I *know*."

I know right now, in this moment, that the decision I make will define the rest of my life. With or without Chris, I have to choose to either move on or hesitate and risk the lives of the rescue team.

I steel my nerves.

And I choose to move on.

The tears will come later.

"Get out of here!" I say. "Move out, let's go!"

I force myself up. The adrenaline of combat keeps my emotions at bay for the time being. We push back through the office. It is actually easier getting out than getting in because of the efficiency of my team – most of the Omega troops are dead and the entrances have been opened on our way inside.

"Manny?" I yell.

To have someone completely disappear during a mission is an anomaly. By the time we reach the other side of the office area, there is a trail of dead Omega troopers in our wake. The frantic scream of the sirens is grating on my nerves. It's times like these that I wish I could simply throw down my gun and make a run for it. Unfortunately, you can't do that if you want to stay alive.

We sweep the stairwell, moving back onto the first floor again. The walls are bathed in red light. I continue to scream Manny's name while we move. Honestly, there's nowhere Manny could really *be* where we wouldn't come across him at some point. It's almost as if he left the building.

And he did it quickly.

Or...he's dead on the floor with countless other Omega troopers.

Please, God. Not Manny, too. Manny's a good man.

I hope God is listening, because nobody else is.

We slam the rear exit doors open and enter the alley. We stick to the plan and retreat around the east side of the alleyway. The airport is clearly visible from here – literally just across the street. Our rendezvous point with Derek is several blocks away from this location. The trick will be *getting* there without being shot.

"Commander!" Uriah says, pointing.

A black helicopter is rumbling to life on the tarmac. Its blades begin to spin – slowly at first, and then faster.

"We should leave," Andrew advises. "Like, now."

I don't disagree. We stick under the cover of the building, rounding the corner. Omega troopers suddenly emerge onto the street. We return with heavy rifle fire, knocking down troops like bowling pins. We retreat back to the opening of the alley. More guards are flooding the street.

"We can go west!" Andrew says.

"If we go west we'll just run into Omega!" I reply.

We can't dash across the airport – there is absolutely no cover there.

Patrols are surrounding us from three sides. Our only escape route is straight ahead of us – the airport. It's surrounded by a chain link fence and barbed wire. Our chances of getting over the fence, running and finding cover are minimal. *Very* minimal. We're trapped.

The helicopter is pounding the air with its blades, obnoxiously loud, even with the sound of gunfire and shouting here at the end of the street. I grimace. We're boxed in on *four* sides, now. Three sides by troops and one side by a combat helicopter.

Still in tight, familiar formation, the few people I have with me tuck in and fight valiantly. I take cover behind the wall of the last building on the block. I am exposed to the clearing of the airport, in addition to being in clear sight of the helicopter. Omega is surrounding us from three sides of the building. We fire and peel back, fire and peel back.

A huge blast rips through the cyclone fence around the tarmac. I drop to the ground, covering my head from pieces of hot metal and flying dirt. The fence springs apart like a slinky. The thundering black helicopter swoops forward, the snouts of the heavy automatic weapons visible from the fuselage.

We are so dead.

"Take cover!" I shout.

Heavy, ripping automatic weapons fire razes downward. It misses us! The trail of thudding bullets whips through the air, taking an Omega patrol out with it. They scream, collapsing, blown apart. I stay where I am, firing and reloading furiously.

The Omega patrols closing in on us from the opposite side of the building scramble to take cover behind the brick walls. The helicopter is hovering about one hundred feet away from our position, but the blast from the blades and the roar of the aircraft itself is tremendous. Enough to knock you off your feet.

The chopper descends and bounces off the asphalt, coming to a harried landing.

"CASSIDY!"

I tilt my head up. The doors on the helicopter are open. Manny is standing in the doorway. He's shouting my name, motioning me with his free hand, his shoulder bloody. In that moment, everything makes sense. It clicks.

"Move it! Everybody in!" I yell, motioning toward the chopper.

We sprint toward the chopper, snapping shots while we run. I feel like I'm clawing my way through a dream. Everything is overwhelmingly loud and each beat of the blades is like a punch in the gut. I reach the door and Uriah helps me climb inside.

"Manny!" I gasp, relief seizing me. He claps me briefly on the shoulder, and pushes his way into the cockpit. His flight cap is strapped tightly to his head and he's grinning devilishly. The team scrambles inside. Vera slaps Manny's arm and gives him the all-clear signal. Then we are airborne, and we are lifting fifty feet off the street.

"There's a wounded POW in the back!" Vera screams.

I can't hear her. I can only read her lips.

"Andrew?" I shout, jerking my thumb toward the back of the chopper.

He nods and makes his way through the aircraft, toward the wounded man in the back.

"Hold on, ladies and gentlemen," Manny yells, still grinning like a madman. "This exit may be a bit bumpy."

The inside of the helicopter is cramped, but we are together – and we are hanging on for dear life.

We gain elevation and bank right and left so fast that I become dizzy and fight the urge to gag. I hang on and hunker down. I see Alexander in the cockpit beside Manny, shouting something that I can't hear.

The urban landscape of Los Angeles flashes past the doorway, but unlike the times that I remember before the EMP, this city is dark. Very few lights can be seen.

The helicopter continues to gain altitude and speed.

Someone grabs my shoulder.

"Cassidy, you're going to want to see this," Andrew says.

"Now is *not* the time to admire the city lights!" I gasp, exasperated.

He maintains his grip on my arm, insisting. The Commander in me kicks in and I realize that Andrew is not that shallow. He must have a reason. We stumble to the back of the chopper. There are two canvas beds on each side. Medical stretchers for the wounded.

Please, don't be somebody I know, I pray.

Andrew looks up at me. In the dim light, he opens his hands as if to offer an apology. He stands up. "He should be okay," he says. He gives me a long, sad look and returns to a more stable position with the rest of the team, gripping the walls for balance. I kneel beside the stretcher. The man is clothed in black, soaked in blood and sweating. I scream.

"Chris?" I brush the hair away from his face. He opens his eyes. Unshaven, drenched in sweat and blood, he stares at the ceiling before turning his gaze to me.

"Cassie...?"

It's barely a whisper, but it's something. I touch his face, placing my hand on his chest. "Oh, my God," I yell into his ear. "Chris? What happened? How...?"

The words die on my lips.

BANG!

The chopper shakes violently and spins through the air.

I clutch the stretcher. Chris is strapped in, but I'm not. I wrap my wrist around the strap of a safety belt. I will not leave his side. Manny shouts something. I can't hear it above the roar of the engine and the air pouring through the opening. Gravity is sucking me sideways, but centrifugal force has pinned me against the floor. Chris is barely conscious, head lolling back and forth.

"I don't have a choice!" I hear Manny yell. Warning lights flash bright. I see orange flames coming from outside.

I brace myself.

We are going down.

Chapter Eleven

I've imagined death so many times. As a soldier, it's
something that you have to think about. I figured I'd be dead on
a battlefield sometime in the next year – if I even lasted that
long. Going down in a flaming helicopter wasn't something I
planned on. First, because I was never crazy about heights. And
second, because I didn't think I'd be riding in a helicopter.

Whatever. Life continually surprises me.

Manny fights for control of the chopper. It spins and
lurches violently in the air. Militiamen and women scream,
terrified. A hole in the side of the fuselage is sucking the
flames and the smoke outside of the aircraft. The chopper
skids sideways. Which way is up? Which way is down? I clutch
the strap on the stretcher, gasping for air. The G-force presses
down on my chest like a weight. Black spots dance before my
eyes as the pressure increases. I can't scream, I can't see. I
can't breathe.

The chopper lurches and everything levels out for a
moment. I swallow some much-needed air. Manny shouts,
"BRACE YOURSELVES!"

I try. I really do. It's not much of a preparation, though. The
chopper slams into the ground. Manny has slowed our
descent enough that the impact doesn't break the helicopter
into pieces – but it still *hurts*. My neck snaps forward. My
wrist is wrapped around the seatbelt strap but it does no
good. My wrist is jerked at an odd angle. I feel the bones grind
together. I don't even have the breath to scream about it.

The chopper bounces roughly, gritting through dirt and trees. Are there buildings here? I don't know. It's too dark. Too loud. The sheer chaos overrides every sense in my body. I hang on with the one functional hand that I have left and slam against the wall. More pain shoots through my body.

This is going to hurt later.

If I'm even *alive* later.

The aircraft begins to slide, tearing apart. The strap that I've been holding onto snaps and I'm thrown against the opposite wall. I protect my head with my arms, landing in a crouched, compact position. The prolonged slide seems to stretch for eternity, but it is only mere seconds.

The giant rotor blades collide with the ground, shards of deadly metal flying everywhere – faster than the speed of a bullet, shredding everything in its path.

I'm thrown back across the chopper. I land on someone's legs. Uriah grabs my shoulders and pulls me upright, offering support. The screaming engine abruptly halts, smoke swirling around us, flames licking through the openings in the chopper.

"Find a hole and get out!" Manny warns.

He manages to climb out of the pilot's seat, rattled by the crash as much as the rest of us. I climb on hands and knees to the medical stretcher again. I unsnap Chris's restraints and drag him out of the bed. He is completely unconscious – and heavy. Superhuman levels of adrenaline is the only reason I have the strength to drag him the first few feet through the helicopter as the team hurriedly exits through the holes. They scramble and tumble outside. I am dragging Chris along with me – using every ounce of strength left in my body.

Uriah suddenly takes Chris's other shoulder and we are dragging him together, outside, into the cold, night air. I stagger out, drop to my knees, and hold my head in my hands. I shake myself and turn back. Uriah and I take Chris further away from the burning helicopter.

I look at my left wrist. It's already turning black and blue. It could be worse.

"Help me get him out of here," I tell Uriah.

Chris groans and a couple of the men carry an empty stretcher out of the helicopter, which is quickly becoming engulfed in flames. This thing is going to be a pain to escape with. We do a quick assessment of our men – a headcount, a check – and hobble to our feet. The enemy is all around us. We are miles away from the Holding Center, but we are still in Los Angeles. If we are able, we should keep moving. We cannot stop. Not yet.

Uriah and Andrew carefully move Chris onto the stretcher. My heart sticks in my throat. I've never seen Chris down and out. Ever. Not like this.

"He's going to be okay," Vera says.

A gesture of comfort? I look at her, smiling sadly.

"I know," I whisper.

The night air is a crisp, welcome change from the sweltering confines of the crashed copter. We're surrounded by trees on all sides.

"Where are we?" I say.

"Looks like a park," Andrew replies. "If we move, we can hide before Omega arrives in full force."

"Okay, we're all accounted for," I say. "We move, we stay hidden, and we work our way back to the rendezvous point to meet with Derek and his team. I want men on point and men on the flank. I want a rear guard." I point to two of the stronger militiamen – tall, burly soldiers. "You carry the stretcher."

I brush the hair away from Chris's forehead. He's burning up.

We start moving. There is no time to waste.

"How did you find him?" I ask quietly.

"Ask yourself a question," Manny replies. He's limping, breathing hard. "If Chris Young and Harry Lydell are both gone at the same time, chances are, they're in the same place, yes?"

"Possibly," I reply.

"When we were moving into the Holding Center," Manny says, "I noticed some activity on the airfield. They were using a POW transport truck and an official Omega vehicle. I thought it might save us all some time if I took the initiative. I was slowing the team down, anyway,"

"I thought you were dead."

"But I wasn't." He winks. "They were moving Young into the chopper. Harry, too, but I didn't see him. I got the feeling that they were transporting him somewhere...more important."

"Why would they transport one officer with a District Prefect?"

"I don't know. Maybe they think Chris is worth it."

"No. *Harry* must have thought it was worth it." I chew on my bottom lip. "God, Manny. If you hadn't stopped that chopper...he'd be gone. Our whole mission would have been a waste."

"Hijacking a helicopter was a piece of cake when Omega's attention was on *you*," Manny cracks. "Besides, it was a whim. Didn't have time to explain it, our deadline was a little too tight, my girl." He briefly puts his arm around my shoulders. "We're still alive."

It's a statement that's meant to cheer me up. I don't feel cheerful. Not yet.

I only feel sweet, complete relief.

Chris is here. He's still alive.

As we push forward through the city park, the distant echo of sirens is audible. Omega is searching for us, and that is exactly what we had expected. They will find the helicopter – a hulking, melted mass of metal – and hopefully assume that we are dead.

If Derek can meet us at our rendezvous point within the next twenty-four hours, we will have survived this thing with almost *all* of our team intact.

Like Andrew said, we can only hope.

Sometimes I think even that is a little too optimistic.

———————————

Beverly Hills, California, is no longer a celebrity city. It's the dwelling place of high-ranking Omega officials. The houses have been taken over by soldiers and patrols. The entire glitzy neighborhood is under control.

We are careful to avoid it.

On our way to the rendezvous point, we pass famous streets like Wilshire Boulevard and Sunset Boulevard. Once swanky apartment buildings where only the elite lived are either being occupied by Omega officials or abandoned altogether. *Millions of Milkshakes*, a celebrity dessert hotspot, is empty. The windows have been blown out. Only the memory remains.

The famed Beverly Hills sign – which, for as long as I can remember, sat in the midst of a green lawn in the middle of the city – is covered with graffiti and smudge marks.

Nothing has escaped Omega's devastating presence.

We head back to Toluca Lake. Twice during our journey we run into Omega patrols, but we outnumber them and we overpower them easily. By the time dawn is breaking over Hollywood Hills, I am bone tired. I can barely lift my feet and keep my eyes open. Each step is robotic. Even the joy of knowing that we have rescued Chris is not enough to energize my body. I am worried that he might not wake up. I am worried that Derek won't make it out of Los Angeles.

Our rendezvous point is a house. A mansion, technically speaking. It's just outside of Toluca Lake, hidden behind a fence overgrown with shrubs and trees.

"Alexander?" I say. "Is this the right place?"

"This is it." He shoves his boot into a crevice and begins pulling himself over the fence. "Start climbing."

"How are we going to get Chris over this thing?" Vera asks, motioning to his still form on the stretcher.

"We'll open the gate," I say simply.

I dig my heels into the brick wall and use the thick foliage and vines to pull myself up. I reach the top of the wall and study the house. It's a large two-story mansion. The entire façade has been overgrown with foliage and twisting vines. It's almost impossible to find the windows.

I swing my legs over the top of the wall. We follow a cobblestone path to the front gate. We unlock it and swing it open. The rest of the militia cautiously moves inside, Uriah and Andrew bringing Chris in on the stretcher.

In the early morning sunlight, Chris's complexion looks pale. Wrong. I press my fingers to his neck, nervously making sure his pulse is still there. It is, and I sigh with relief.

"Check it out," I tell my team.

Wounded and exhausted, I let Uriah and Alexander lead the recon team around and inside the mansion, making sure there are no signs of Omega or unsavory individuals. The scouts report back, and Alexander gives the all-clear signal.

I cradle my aching wrist. It's swollen, black and blue. Every step brings a throbbing sensation of pain. We pass the threshold of the front door. It's cold inside. Musty, dusty. Dark. Rooms full of expensive, dusty furniture. Two sets of stairwells separate from the main hall, leading to an ornate second level.

"Take Chris upstairs, into one of the bedrooms," I say. "I'm going to need a medic." I pause. "Or two."

"Roger that, Commander," Andrew replies.

"Manny, you tend to that shoulder," I command.

He winces, but still offers a smile.

"Yes, ma'am," he says.

"And Manny?"

He raises an eyebrow.

"Thank you for getting us out of there," I tell him. "You saved our lives."

I wrap my arms around his neck and give him a warm hug. An exhausted hug. One filled with relief and gratitude and disbelief – yes, we're still alive. Really. Manny smells like sweat and smoke and fuel. He gently returns the hug, then steps away.

"It was a pleasure, my girl," he murmurs, watching the men haul Chris on the stretcher up the stairs. "Just make sure he wakes up."

"I will," I say.

I turn and follow Chris's still form up the stairwell. After the record-breaking adrenaline of the last few hours, I feel like I'm coming down from an epic high. It's like getting hit by a truck.

"Here is fine," I say, motioning to a bedroom on the left. This must have been the master bedroom. There's a huge bed, a massive dresser and closet, and the carpet is soft beneath my feet. Too soft. I feel like I'm ruining it.

They lay Chris on the bed. I take a seat on the edge and slip my fingers through his. He doesn't twitch. He only breathes in and out. In and out. He hasn't woken again since the helicopter went down.

I press a soft kiss against his forehead.

"Please, wake up," I whisper. "I love you."

At this point, my prayers are all I have left.

Chapter Twelve

"My brother isn't big on romantic stuff," Jeff Young says. "It's kind of a wonder that he is the way he is with you."

"I don't know if that's a good thing," I reply. "I feel like he loves me, but I don't know. He doesn't talk about that kind of stuff. He just...*is*."

"Yeah, that's Chris," Jeff agrees, laughing. He's such a good boy. Good looking, funny, caring, sympathetic. Where Chris is rough, Jeff is sweet, and where Chris won't discuss things, Jeff opens right up. They are, in so many ways, like night and day. And yet they're alike.

"Do you think he cares?" I ask Jeff. I rest my hands on my knees. We've been in Sector 20 for two weeks now, and we're about to roll out to the Chokepoint to face Omega's five-million man army. Both of us are young, nervous and afraid.

"Cares about what?" he replies.

"About me. Do you think he really cares?"

"Come on, Cassidy. Of course he cares. He wouldn't have made an effort to rescue you from the labor camp if he didn't care," he says. "He wouldn't be here now."

"I don't want him to stay with me out of some kind of moral obligation to keep me safe," I sigh. "I want him to want this."

Jeff grins, and he takes both my hands in his.

"Cassidy, my brother loves you," he says. "He doesn't say it, but he shows it. You and I both know that."

I press my forehead against Jeff's and take a deep breath.

"If we get out of this alive," I promise, "you and I are going to be besties."

"We already are, Cassidy." He kisses my cheek. "We've always been."

I wake up suddenly, the memory slash dream ringing clearly in my brain. Jeff Young is dead. He's no longer around for me to confide in. I close my eyes and burrow into the warmth of the pillow, the blankets soft around my shoulders. My wrist is wrapped in thick bandages. It's painful, but necessary.

"Cassie." I feel his breath on my neck before I feel his touch. "Hey, I know you're awake."

I open my eyes and look up, flat on my back. Chris is looking down at me. His face is weary, but he's smiling. It's a beautiful sight. His green eyes – those vibrant, electric green eyes – are ringed with pain and tiredness. But he's awake. And alive.

"Chris!"

For the first time in *forever*, I explode with joy. I haven't been this happy since I found my father earlier this year. I fling my arms around Chris's neck and cry, sobbing out of sheer relief and happiness. He presses his fingers against my waist and kisses my neck. "It's okay," he says. "Cassie, it's okay. Don't cry. Shhh."

But when I pull away and study his face, there are tears in his eyes, too.

"What happened?" I whisper.

"War happened," he replies. He gently brushes his lips across my cheeks, catching my tears with his thumbs. "You crazy girl. You shouldn't have come all this way for me."

"I wasn't alone," I reply, holding him tightly. I love the way it feels to be in his arms again. I feel safe. Whole. "Everyone here came of their own free will."

"So you didn't bribe anybody into it?" he smiles.

"Ha. No." I kiss his forehead, his cheeks. "Oh, my God, Chris. I missed you. I was so worried. I thought you were dead." I start to cry again. "I thought I'd never see you again."

"I know, sweetheart. I'm sorry." He holds me close, rubbing comforting circles into the small of my back. "You're amazing, you know that?" My head sinks into the pillow. He gazes at me with an incredibly gentle expression. "Why did you do this, Cassie? You didn't have to."

"Yes, I did." I trace my finger along his jaw. "I love you. You came for me when I was imprisoned. It was my turn to come for you. I wasn't going to let you die."

"You should have." Chris looks sad. "You put yourself in unnecessary danger."

"That can't be helped. Not anymore."

"It can be helped if I have anything to do with it."

"Well, you were a POW, and you didn't have anything to do with it." I laugh. "They voted me Commander. Can you believe that? Me. How weird is that?"

"Not weird at all," Chris replies solemnly. "It's always been in you."

"Everyone that came with me," I say, "are all here because they believe in you. They respect you. Because we need you *back.*"

"I'm here now." He presses soft, lingering kisses along my shoulder. "What happened to your wrist?"

"I sprained it."

"I can see that. How?"

"Bumpy helicopter rides. Always wear a seatbelt."

He chuckles. "I'm sorry." He kisses my fingers. "Cassie, how did you get me out of the Holding Center? I don't remember anything."

"Maybe we should cover that later," I say, pulling his head down to mine. "Just kiss me."

He laughs.

"Fair enough," he agrees.

It's a good agreement. The best one I've had in a long time.

––––––––––––––

Our wait at the rendezvous point can only last for so long. Eventually we will have to move on. I hope Derek shows up soon. The longer we wait here, the more of a chance Omega has of finding us.

Chris's head is in my lap. We're sitting in the couch in the back of the bedroom. His wounds have been tended to by the medics. He was suffering from a concussion, extensive bruising from the beatings and torture of Omega interrogation, malnutrition and extreme dehydration when Manny found him in the POW truck outside of the helicopter at the Holding Center. We've been at the rendezvous point for six hours, now. Most of the militia team is asleep. We're exhausted, and most are wounded to one degree or another. If we want to have enough strength to make it back over the Tehachapi Mountains, this is a necessary rest.

"Tell me everything," I encourage Chris, twisting his hair around my fingers.

"It's not pleasant, Cassidy," he replies.

"I think that's obvious." I dip my head down and kiss the tip of his nose. "I didn't come all this way for you to keep things from me. You don't need to protect me anymore. Those days are over."

He gazes up, capturing my hand.

"Yeah," he says sadly. "I guess they are." Silence hangs between us before he finally begins. "Back at the Chokepoint, when I sent you into the drainpipe with Jeff and Sophia," he starts, "I *was* right behind you. It was just one of those things. I was shot in the shoulder. Here." He pulls down the collar of his dark blue tee shirt. There's the bright red scar of a recent wound. "It nailed me. I just couldn't make it fast enough. I'm sorry."

I stare at the ceiling.

One of the worst moments of my life was realizing that Chris wasn't following me out of the battlefield – that I was returning to base without him. It was a nightmare.

"What about Max?" I ask softly.

Chris stayed behind to help Max, our resident explosive professional, after he had been wounded. Uriah abandoned both of them on the field. It's for that reason I've had such a hard time forgiving Uriah for his cowardice. You could almost say that it was *his* fault that Chris was captured.

"Max is dead, Cassie," Chris whispers. "There was nothing I could do."

I close my eyes. Tears burn like acid in the back of my throat.

Goodbye, Max. You were a good man. You saved my life once.

"I know," Chris says, stroking his thumb across my hand. "I'm sorry. Believe me, nobody's more sorry than I am." He lets the horrible news sink in for a moment before continuing, "I was pretty banged up. All I know is that they didn't kill me outright because they knew who I was. Harry gave orders to take me alive, if possible." He shrugs. "Next thing I know, I'm beaten, knocked down, tied up and in a truck headed south. By the time I was halfway conscious, I was in a cell in the Holding Center. Ten by ten room, no windows, standard jail cell." He sighs. "Harry's motives for keeping me alive are a lot more personal than they are critical to Omega's war effort."

"He wanted revenge," I state. "He always hated you for showing him up when we were camped in the mountains. He hated me, too."

"No, I don't think he hates you," Chris replies. "I think he wanted you dead merely for the purpose of exacting revenge on me. He knew it would kill me if anything happened to you."

"Why was he so obsessed?" I ask.

"Selfish pride," he says. "Ego. Maybe a little bit of insanity." He shrugs. "Does it matter? He interrogated me for a week on militia strategy and battle plans. I didn't give him anything except false leads and nonsense. Nothing."

"Of course you didn't," I smile. It's a sad smile, though. "I'm sorry."

"It is what it is," he answers. "I think he realized I was worthless to him for information, but I still made good bait. That's when he moved me to a different cell. I was in there for almost a week...I think. It's hard to say."

"Manny found you in the end," I say. "He saw the POW transport truck on the tarmac. If it wasn't for him, we never would have found you in time."

"Harry was leaving?" Chris looks puzzled. "That son of a...he wasn't kidding."

"What are you talking about?"

"He kept talking about going 'up north,' to some Omega gathering," he explains. "He was hoping to have both of us there. As trophies of war, maybe. The founders of the militia groups in the central valley? It might have scored him extra points with the high ranking Omega officers."

"Up north?" I wonder. "I wonder where he was going?"

"I don't know." He shakes his head. "He was taking me with him? That doesn't make sense."

"It does if you're an egotistical sociopath," I say. "You're right. He was probably hoping to use both of us to earn brownie points. A public execution would have gotten him another promotion." I slam my fist against the couch's armrest. "I don't understand. There's got to be more to this picture than what we're seeing. This isn't right. It's just...there must have been a good reason. More than just revenge."

"I don't know." Chris nuzzles my waist, drawing me closer. "Thank you."

"For...?"

"For being you," he says. He sits up slowly, drawing me close to his chest. "There aren't a lot of women that would do this for a man."

"You're not just any man." I lean my cheek against his skin, listening to his steady heartbeat. "And this isn't just any normal situation. This is war. And I love you, Chris. There wasn't a question of *if* we could come for you. It was *when*."

"I know," he laughs. "Like I was saying. You're one of a kind."

He kisses me. Deeply, heavily. It's a kiss of relief and desperation and hope – all of those things wrapped into one. He gently squeezes my hips and I sit on my knees, my hands tangled in his hair.

"Cassie," he says softly, cupping the back my head in his hand. "There's something you need to know. I'd rather tell you now..."

"Tell me what?"

"Just-"

Someone knocks on the door. I bolt upright, flushed with color, breathing hard. Chris grins and pulls me back to him. I laugh softly and kiss his cheek one last time.

"Commander?" It's Uriah's voice. "Derek and his team made it."

Thank God!

I get to my feet and open the bedroom door. Uriah's eyes are wide as he assesses me, red cheeks and all. Chris is lounging on the couch. He gets up – slowly – and walks to the door. He's a good four inches taller than Uriah. That doesn't take the hurt out of Uriah's eyes, though, seeing the two of us together.

"He's okay," Uriah reports quietly. "He's downstairs."

He pauses, then,

"Nice to see you back, Commander Young." Uriah nods respectfully. He looks between us a few times, doing the math. "Congratulations, Cassidy."

"Who came on this mission?" Chris asks.

"All militiamen," I reply. "Vera, Derek, Manny, Uriah, Me..." I shrug. "Everybody. Alexander's alive. He's here, too."

"What about Sophia?" he says, leveling his gaze at me.

"She...chose not to come."

"Where you go, she goes."

"She made her choice."

"I'll meet you downstairs," Uriah says. He slowly retreats, but not before giving me a baleful expression. One that makes me feel guilty.

"She was wounded?" Chris presses.

"She was...hurt emotionally." I say. "After Alexander went MIA and Jeff-"

"-What about Jeff?" Chris' eyes flash. And that's when a horrible realization hits home.

Chris doesn't know.

He doesn't know that his little brother is dead.

"Chris," I breathe. "I...I don't know how to tell you this."

"Tell me what?" He stares at me, waiting. And then he starts to shake his head. "No. Not Jeff."

"I'm sorry." Tears, hot and salty, pool in my eyes. "He died in my arms."

He stares at the wall, a muscle ticking in his jaw. I don't dare touch him.

"We were retreating," I explain, my voice trembling. "We were in the drainpipe. There was nothing I could do. I tried, I swear. I tried." I bite my lip. I know Chris, and the best thing I can do is leave him alone while he digests this news. "He died fighting, Chris. He died like a man." I place both hands on his face and give him a soft kiss. "I'm sorry. I'm so sorry."

What else can I say? What is someone *supposed* to say when someone you love dies? Nothing can be done about it. Nothing can be changed. There is no fix. It's final. It's over.

Chris doesn't speak.

I respect his silence and slip into the hall. I need to give him some time. Chris loved his brother. He did everything he could to protect him. And now Jeff is dead, and Chris's heart has been broken.

"He didn't know, did he?" Uriah is standing at the bottom of the staircase. The room is empty. The gentle murmur of voices can be heard in the living room. I shake my head. Uriah folds his arms across his chest, oozing tall, dark, and brooding – like always.

"Look," he says. "Will you promise me something?"

"Depends on the promise."

"Don't tell Chris about...my feelings toward you."

I raise an eyebrow. "Why?" I say. "You don't think he'd like finding out that you kissed me? Without asking?"

Uriah flinches.

"I really care about you, Cassidy," he whispers, stepping closer. "And I don't want that to be ruined. Please, don't tell him. Not because I'm afraid of getting my butt kicked by a SEAL, but because I care about you. I want us to be friends."

I contemplate this.

"You should have tried being my friend *first*," I remark. "But I don't mind starting over if you don't."

He smiles. One of the few times Uriah True has ever done so.

"Okay, then," he says. "To friendship?"

He offers his hand.

"To friendship," I agree. "You're a good guy, Uriah."

In this moment, I realize that I may have not completely forgiven Uriah for what he has done...but I can forgive myself for everything that's happened. I don't need to feel guilty about losing Chris on the battlefield anymore. The problem has been dealt with. Chris is here.

It's time to let it go.

"Should we, um, go see Derek?" he asks, clearing his throat.

"Sure." I grin. "Don't get awkward on me, Uriah. Friends aren't awkward."

"Well, I could debate that..."

I laugh.

We walk into the living room. It's a wide space with a pool table. Militiamen and women are lying on the couches, resting. Gas lanterns give the room light. Derek is standing near the fireplace. He's smudged in grease and dirt, but he looks fine. "Derek," I exclaim. I embrace him. "Are you okay?"

"Yes ma'am," he replies. "I hear our objective was achieved."

"It was." I pause. "Did you have any trouble getting back?"

"Some harassing fire. Some diversions. Nothing we couldn't handle. Omega was busy searching the skies for you," he says. "We're faster than they were. We were ahead of the patrols."

"Good."

Vera taps me on the shoulder. She looks tired.

"Cassidy, can we talk?" she asks.

What is it with everybody and their brother wanting to *talk*?

I nod.

"Be right back," I tell Derek. "Glad to see you made it back safely."

"Same to you, Commander."

I follow Vera out of the crowded area, into an empty dining room. There is almost no light here. Vera's skin is pale, her hair is filthy and her clothes are dirty. Yet she still looks pretty, and in the past, that would have eaten at me. Why should she look great in the middle of an apocalypse while I look like something the cat dragged in?

I've come to a point, I guess, where I simply don't *care* anymore.

I'm alive. Chris is alive. That is all that matters.

"Cassidy, what I'm about to tell you is just between the two of us," she says.

I ask, "Is something wrong?"

"Nothing's wrong. I just...here's the thing, Hart. I came out here with this rescue unit," she continues, "and now we've found Chris, and we're going to head back to the National Guard base in Fresno. Happily ever after, right?"

"It's a far cry from happily ever after, but yeah," I shrug. "What's your point?"

"My point is, I was *wrong*, okay?" she tenses. "You're a good commander. And...yeah. That's basically what I wanted to say." She tosses her hair back. "I'm glad we've got Chris back."

"Me too." I raise an eyebrow, suspecting a trick. "So that's all. You just wanted to tell me that I was a good commander?"

"Yeah." She picks at the sleeve of her jacket. "And...Cassidy, I think you should know something. About Chris."

My heartbeat picks up. I don't know why. Maybe it's because Vera has nursed an ill-concealed crush on Chris for as long as she's known him. Or maybe because there's something in her voice that seems oddly emotional.

Emotional for Vera, anyway.

"He was married," she says.

I blink.

"What are you *talking* about?"

"My mother," she continues. "She was in the Navy in San Diego. She knew Chris Young before the EMP. Chris was married before everything went down. He never told you that, did he?"

I stare at her. I feel ill. *Very,* very ill.

"You're joking," I say. "Stop it."

"I'm not joking, Hart." She shakes her head. "I'm sorry. It's just been...it's been on my mind, okay? I don't know why. I was never going to tell you because honestly, I didn't care about you. But now...things are different. You deserve to know."

"I don't believe you," I state.

"I'm not lying. Ask him."

"You're saying Chris *is* married or *was* married?"

"I don't know. I just know that my mother knew who he was, and he was married at the time." She's wearing an expression of frustration. "I don't know the details. I just know what my mother told me."

"I still don't believe you," I say.

I turn to walk away. Vera grabs my arm. I give her a warning look.

Don't touch me.

She's not as stupid as she used to be. She lets go and takes a step back.

"I'm not lying," she presses.

I ignore her and walk away.

There are a lot of things I can handle.

This is not one of them.

Chapter Thirteen

I was born into a broken marriage. My parents divorced when I was a child. The separation was the healthiest thing that could have happened for me. I was no longer exposed to constant bickering or screaming contests. Suddenly, there were no noises in the house. Only empty silence.

It was different. But it was good.

I remember telling myself that I would never get married. I never wanted to deal with the heartbreak and humiliation of divorce. I never wanted to live like that. I wanted normalcy and stability, and for that I was convinced that I could depend on nobody but *myself*.

When society collapsed, I acted independently to find my father, but in the process, became very dependent on Chris Young for survival. Depending on someone for survival is one thing – depending on them for happiness is an entirely different matter. It has taken a long time to extricate myself from the web of dependence I entangled myself within. Where I used to hesitate, I'm confident, and where I was once petty, I simply don't *care* anymore.

But the bombshell that Vera dropped on me rocked the foundation of my relationship with Chris. If what she says is true, then there really *is* a lot that I don't know about the man I'm in love with. Maybe the real question that's bouncing around inside my head is this: *Why didn't Chris tell me himself? Was he **ever** planning on telling me, or was he going to keep it a secret for the rest of his life? Or is there any truth to the story?*

At any rate, my stomach is a writhing mess. I'm pacing at the front door, waiting for the militia to gather their gear. We've been here for twenty-four hours. Omega hasn't found us, and it's time for us to begin our journey back to Arlene's Way House in the Tehachapi Mountains.

I haven't spoken to Chris since I told him that his brother was dead.

I have barely been able to deal with the pain of that loss myself. Focusing on rescuing Chris was the only thing that kept me together. Now that I've achieved my goal, the loss hurts like a fresh wound.

"Are you okay, Cassidy?" Uriah asks.

He's sitting on the steps, cleaning his rifle.

"Yeah," I say, clearing my throat. "Just tired. You?"

"Same." I can tell that he doesn't buy it. "What did Vera say to you?"

"Nothing."

I say it a little too quickly. Uriah stands up and slings his rifle over his shoulder. He walks closer, smiling faintly. "Cassidy," he says. "Whatever it is, remember that you've got people here who really care about you. You're not alone."

"Thank you," I reply.

Footsteps on the stairwell snap me out of it. I take a reflexive step backward and meet Chris's gaze. He's wearing black combat pants and a black shirt. He's leaner than he was a few weeks ago – a side effect of suffering torturous interrogation and malnutrition. He's shaved the excess scruff from his face and pulled his hair back into a tight ponytail. He has eaten a couple of times since he's been here, but he'll need more food if he's going to get his full strength back.

"True," Chris says, giving Uriah a stony expression.

"Commander," Uriah replies, saluting. "Good to see that you made it, sir."

Chris looks between us and I realize that I have unconsciously taken another step backward. Despite our earlier conversation about being friends, Uriah seems incredibly uncomfortable under Chris's glare. Uriah excuses himself, mumbling something about checking on the militiamen in the living room.

Chris raises an eyebrow. I shrug.

He kisses me quickly on the forehead, brushing his hand on my hip. The two of us head to the living room. The militiamen are geared up and ready to go. Manny is sitting on the couch. His leather coat has been stitched up at the shoulder, where the bullet pierced the clothing...and skin. He's a bit pale, but other than that, he looks better. Healthier.

"Manny," I say, taking his hand. "How are you feeling?"

"Like a million dollars," he replies, grinning widely. "I should get shot more often. I've been told I'm a miracle fast-healer."

"I believe it," Chris says.

"Chris Young." Manny stands up, grasping Chris's hand. "My boy. Welcome back."

"Thank you." He claps Manny on the shoulder. "Nice work with the helicopter, Manny. Good job."

"It was impressive, if I do say so myself."

"Commander," Derek exclaims. "Good to see you back, sir."

The two men embrace briefly. Of everyone here, Derek has been with Chris's militia the longest. Even before I joined. Except for...

Alexander Ramos.

He's standing near the fireplace, his arms crossed over his chest. A hush falls over the room when Chris approaches. Two men – both of them thought dead. Both of them survived. And both of them, begrudging allies and now friends.

"Ramos," Chris says.

And that's it. They shake hands, embrace for a moment and nod respectfully. It's a solemn moment of recognition. They both care about each other, even if they won't say it out loud.

"Welcome back, Commander," Vera says.

She's seated on the couch armrest near Manny. Chris acknowledges her words with a brief tilt of his head. For some reason I find it extremely satisfying. And then the room practically hums with unspoken words as Chris stands in the middle of the group of militiamen and women.

"I want to thank you for what you've done," Chris says. "A rescue unit in the heart of an Omega stronghold? Suicide. But here you stand, successful. It is my honor to be your Commander. I couldn't ask for better soldiers." He looks directly at me. "Some of you have performed above and beyond expectations. Thank you. This war has not torn us apart. It's brought us closer together. We know what we want now: we want our lives back. And it's given us drive and motivation. You wouldn't be here if you didn't believe in the promise of freedom as much as I do. I want you to know that everything you do is worthwhile. Every drop of blood that has been spilled is not in vain. There is a purpose. There is an end goal." He stops to clench his fists, and I know that he is thinking of his brother. "And God willing, we will be victorious."

"Amen to that," Manny drawls, slapping his hands together. "What do you say we pack up and head home, Commander?"

"Yes," Chris and I reply at the same time.

Force of habit.

Chris's lips twitch.

"Yes," he says again. "What we said."

I leave the room and climb the stairwell, heading to the bedroom. I gather my gear as quickly as possible, checking my weapons and ammunition. A million emotions are swirling inside of my head:

Relief:

We survived the rescue mission into Los Angeles.

Confusion:

What is Chris not telling me about his past life?

Fear:

What will I have to deal with when we return to Fresno?

I sense Chris's presence before he even steps into the room. I look up quickly, hands trembling as I zip my backpack shut. "Are you feeling good enough to head back?" I ask. "You were pretty beat up when we got here."

"I'm a fighter," Chris replies, gently grasping my waist from behind. "And so are you, Cassie. Everything's going be fine. You know that. Hang onto that hope."

I want to say, *Vera told me something that's driving me crazy!*

But I don't. Not yet.

Chris places his hands over mine, closing his fingers over my trembling fists. He kisses the side of my neck, locking me into an inescapable embrace. His breath tickles my ear. "What's bothering you?" he whispers. "Something's not right."

"I'm just tired," I say. "It's been a long two weeks."

"It has."

I study his hands. For the first time, I notice the angry red lines crisscrossing his wrists. The scars of torture. I close my eyes, silently thanking God that we found Chris before he was executed.

"Was he horrible?" I ask.

"Who?"

"Harry. Did he do this to you?" I touch his hands.

"Harry didn't lift a finger," Chris replies. "He has people for this."

"I'm so sorry, Chris."

"Don't be. It's the price of being in charge."

"Nobody deserves torture."

He doesn't answer. He just kisses me again.

"If I could go back," I say, "I wouldn't have gone into that stupid drainpipe. I would have made Jeff go ahead of me and I would have come back for you."

"You can't change the past, Cassie," Chris answers, his voice gentle. "Don't live in that place. It will destroy you. Believe me, I know." He turns me around and tilts my chin up, meeting my eyes. "We could go over every scenario a thousand times and think of ways that we could have changed things, but it still *wouldn't* change anything. So don't look behind you. Keep moving forward."

Looking at Chris, I realize that *this* is the reason I fell in love with him.

Not because of his good looks. Not because of his fighting capabilities. Not because of his leadership skills. But because he is a good man. A man of integrity and honor and respect.

This is why I came to Los Angeles and risked my life.

"I will keep moving forward," I say.

And for the time being, I put Vera's words out of my mind. Chris is mine, now.

It's time to stop living in the past.

We get lucky. We leave Toluca Lake and the rendezvous point at midnight. The streets are dark and cold. There are no lights. It's amazing to me how a city that was once full of noise and light is now so dark and empty. It's literally nothing but a husk of what it was.

Chris leads the group, and it is obvious how glad everyone is to have him back. *This* is what we came here for. We came for our leader, we found him, and everything is right with the world.

Well. What's *left* of the world, anyway.

We slip through abandoned streets in unit formation. At one point I stop to look at a limousine sitting at the curb. It's rusted over. Weeds twist around the wheels. The rear windows are missing. Dried blood is caked to the exterior of the doors.

I jog to catch up with Chris.

"Did Alexander tell you about Mexico?" I ask.

"Yeah," he replies.

"And...?"

"And what?"

"What's your theory? I know you have one."

He smirks.

"If Mexico *is* fighting Omega," he says, "then that's good news for us. It'll take the pressure off."

"What about China? They'll be back."

"They will."

I sigh.

"I wish we could just turn on the news and get all of the information," I say. "Don't you miss that?"

"The news was nothing but part of the truth, anyway," Chris shrugs. "This isn't that much different. It's just slower."

"You're such a conspiracy theorist."

"Right. *I'm* a conspiracy theorist."

I playfully nudge his shoulder, but not *too* hard.

He *is* our Commander, after all.

"So," I begin again. "The Mad Monks. We might run into them on the way home. They're actually on our side. The rumors are exaggerated."

"I suspected as much."

"They helped us navigate to Toluca Lake on our way in. They knew who you were."

"Even in wartime people gossip."

"No. You're just *really* popular," I whisper.

He shakes his head, but I know he's smiling.

By the time we make it out of Toluca Lake, it's been a few hours. We climb to the top of the far mountain – the same mountain where we entered the city. Twilight has settled over the horizon, casting an eerie gray pallor over the skyline. The ravaged ruins of the skyscrapers look like something out of a horror movie.

"It's something, isn't it?" Manny remarks.

"It *was*," I say, sad.

"It will be again," Chris interjects, his eyes focused on something in the distance. "Come on."

He doesn't linger. We slip over the ridgeline before sunrise, disappearing into the golden grass of the hills.

Goodbye, Los Angeles.

We will meet again someday.

Chapter Fourteen

We reunite with our horses. The Underground militia
operatives are waiting for us at a Way House in the hills. It's a
small ranch house, surrounded by trees. The stable in the
back is hidden from the air. We move out quickly. Chris talks
to the operatives and I find my way into the stable. It smells
like wet hay and animals. It's a familiar, comforting scent.

"Katana!"

Her gorgeous, velvety fur practically glows in the early
morning sunlight. She recognizes me instantly. I kiss her soft
nose and scratch her behind the ears.

"Hey, girl," I whisper. "We made it back in one piece. It's a
miracle."

It doesn't take us long to gear up. Mach – the midnight
black horse that was previously Uriah's mount – is chosen by
Chris. He swings himself into the saddle with ease. Is there
anything that he *can't* do?

Nope. He can do everything.

I adjust to Katana's rhythmic movement as we hit the trail.
I've missed traveling by horseback, honestly. It's fun – and a
lot faster than walking. Even if it *does* make me saddle sore.

I trot Katana alongside Chris's horse as we journey along
the trails. I keep my eyes open for signs of the Mad Monks, but
everything is oddly quiet. There are no footprints, no areas of
broken grass. I have trained myself to look for irregularities in
natural landscapes – signs of human life. But here, I see

nothing. And that disturbs me. If this is Mad Monk territory, I should have spotted something by now.

Right?

If Chris feels the same way, he says nothing. Instead he's just eternally alert, watchful and cautious. In other words, he's *Chris.* I feel incredibly relieved to not have to be the number one person in charge anymore, although we still maintain our security formation, and I am always watching for trouble.

We camp when it gets dark and rest. I sleep on the ground near Katana, my head propped up on my backpack. The weather is getting colder. It's nearly November, now. Almost one year since the EMP destroyed the world as we knew it.

Not even a year. Wow.

I see Chris talking to Alexander. They're speaking in hushed tones while the militia drifts off to sleep, just out of earshot of the soldiers keeping watch.

I fall asleep. Morning comes way too quickly. We saddle up and get moving again. The following days are uneventful. Peaceful, even. I wonder why we couldn't have had this kind of experience on the way *in* to Los Angeles. I mean, we were actually in a hurry *then*!

That's life, I guess.

By the time we make our way back to Arlene's Way House, everyone in the militia is numbed with exhaustion. It has been almost three weeks since we left the National Guard to rescue Chris. In that timespan we have lost four soldiers, penetrated the heart of Omega's stronghold and rescued Chris – along with about a dozen other militia officers. Our mission has been a success, despite the casualties that we took. It's the first time in a long time that something has actually gone *right.*

It gives me a little bit of hope.

The trees surrounding Arlene's house have paled in color since we were last here. Winter is coming. Dead leaves crackle and twigs snap beneath the horses' hooves. I stay on Katana and watch the bushes and shrubs. The fact that I was nearly attacked by a German Shepherd the last time I was here has not been forgotten.

"Notice something?" I whisper suddenly.

"What?" Vera asks. She pulls up on her horse beside me.

"There are no dogs."

The fence around the front of the house is empty. The sign that reads NO TRESPASSING is gone. I twist my head around and look at Manny. He's sitting motionless on his horse, a concerned expression on his face.

"That's not right," I mutter.

I slide my legs over Katana's back and land on the dirt. Chris does the same.

"What should we have been expecting?" Chris asks me, raising an eyebrow.

"Well...not this." I shake my head. "This is too quiet. And the sign..."

Manny dismounts, followed by Uriah, Vera, Andrew, Derek, Alexander and the rest of the militia. I am the first one through the wire gate. It creaks loudly, unlocked. I grip a small handgun. Yet again, we are scoping out another perimeter. Looking for an enemy. I look at Chris. I look at Uriah.

I say, "Do a quick recon of the house. Make sure nobody's hiding here."

Uriah nods. Both he and Derek take some militiamen and fan out around the house, searching the property for signs of trouble. I stare at the front door.

It's standing wide open.

"Arlene," Manny breathes.

He rushes to the front door and steps inside the house. Chris and I are right on his heels. The furniture in the front hallway has been smashed. The mirror on the far wall in the living room is shattered. Bits of glass are strewn across the floor, glittering in the early morning sunlight. A cold chill slides down my spine.

This is bad.

"Search the house," Chris commands.

Manny pushes his way into the living room.

"Arlene?" he calls. "Arlene?"

We search the kitchen, the bedrooms, the dining room – even the basement. There is no sign of life. "Commander?" Derek appears at the front door.

"Well?" Chris says.

"You need to see this."

Dread seizes me. Those five words never hold a positive meaning.

Never.

Chris and I walk outside, following Derek around the edge of the house. Manny is with us. The stench of death is sickening. In the backyard, near the stables, the bodies of five dead dogs are laid in a straight line. I cover my mouth to keep from gagging. Dried blood is splattered on the sidewalk. Flies buzz around the carcasses. Chris places his hand on my shoulder.

I pray to God that Arlene's body isn't here, too.

"She's not here," Derek says, looking at Manny. "There's no sign of her."

"Doesn't mean she's not dead, too," Uriah mutters.

"She might have escaped," Manny states. His skin is ashen – the first time I have *ever* seen him so upset. "I know Arlene. She would have found a way to get out."

"Who did this?" Vera asks, taking a disgusted step back from the dead dogs. "Mercenaries? Omega?"

"This was meant to look like a gang did this," Manny says. He points to graffiti on the far wall of the back patio.

"But they didn't." Chris gives my shoulder a squeeze. "They didn't take anything. They didn't loot the property. What they broke inside the house was a result of some kind of a fight. Maybe Arlene had friends with her when it happened. They fought back."

"Do you know where Arlene might have gone?" I ask.

"No idea," Manny replies. "But I don't care, as long as she's alive."

"In the meantime, what do we do with these horses?" Vera asks.

"Our vehicles are still hidden here," Derek reports to Chris. "Well hidden. Whoever attacked here completely missed them."

"Thank God," I say. "But yeah. The horses. What do we do with them?"

"We leave them here," Derek says. "We've got to get back to the National Guard. We don't have a choice."

"They'll die uncared for."

"No, they won't," Manny interjects. "There's plenty of water and grazing land around here to keep them comfortable."

I lower myself into a crouch on the ground, resting my arms on my knees. The stables haven't been touched, and it looks as if most of the property is still intact. It could have been worse...I suppose.

"This house is a vital part of our communication with the Underground," Manny points out. "We can't leave it abandoned."

"So what? We leave someone behind to take care of the horses?"

"Until the Underground can replace them, yes."

"Who wants to volunteer?"

Silence. Yeah. That's what I thought. Nobody.

"I will."

I don't know this man. He is one of the twelve officers we rescued from the Holding Center in Los Angeles. He's unshaven – maybe forty years old. His eyes are bloodshot. He looks weary.

"One man and thirty horses isn't going to be enough," I say.

"How about twelve men?" He gestures to the officers around them. "We've been rotting in the Holding Center for almost six months, Commander Hart. We'll be glad to do anything the militia needs us to do until they can send a replacement team."

"You're officers, though," Vera says. "Valuable."

"Doesn't matter. We're all on the same level now."

"There's a nice hidden stash of heavy weaponry on the property," Manny says suddenly, stroking his jaw. "You boys would have everything you need to hold down the fort."

I glance at Chris. I can see that he is considering it.

"The Underground would have someone to replace you in about a week," Chris says. "Can you survive that long?"

"We will do our best, sir."

"Hey, guys!" Andrew bursts out of the house. He's holding a radio set and speakers. He sets it on the table. I turn away from the stench of the dead dogs. "You're not going to believe this."

"What?"

"I found Arlene's radio. It was in her bedroom, hidden." He pauses and turns the volume up. There's a steady sheet of static before a short burst of dialogue:

"Safe District, this is Hammer Point." A man's voice. Everyone holds their breath, staring.

"Roger that, Hammer Point," Andrew replies, talking into the receiver. "Repeat."

"Yes, sir," the voice answers. "I repeat: San Diego District is now under Mexican control. They have taken the city. Omega is pulling back into Los Angeles. The Pacific Northwest Alliance has gained a foothold in Northern California, including San Francisco. Rebel forces are converging in Sacramento. I repeat, *Sacramento*."

"Sacramento?" I whisper.

"Pacific Northwest Alliance?" Uriah says.

"What's the RV point in Sacramento?" Andrew asks.

"You'll be given that information at a later time," the voice says.

"A later time?" I echo.

"Thank you, Hammer Point," Andrew says. "Over and out."

I look at Chris.

"Who's Hammer Point?" I ask.

"Underground radio in Los Angeles," Alexander answers for him. "The Way House where we stayed on the way into the city."

"So this Pacific Northwest Alliance is attacking Omega up north, Mexico is attacking from the south, and the National Guard is defending the central valley," Vera states. "God, I hope Mexico and Canada are on our side."

"He said rebel forces were massing in Sacramento," Uriah says. "What does that mean?"

"It means things just got a lot more serious," Chris replies. "Omega's push on the west coast has stalled, and somebody's finally got enough sense to unite the militia forces in Sacramento."

"What about-"

I'm cut off by the radio.

"Safe District, this is Halo Four." The voice is female.

Manny jumps up and grabs the radio.

"Arlene," he breathes. "This is Safe District."

"I heard you call in from Safe District and I knew it had to be you," she replies. There is relief in her voice – and in Manny's.

"What happened to you?" he asks.

"Mercenaries," she replies. "They attacked about four days after you left. I escaped and now I'm at Halo Point with some of my people, waiting for orders."

"Where's Halo Point?" Vera whispers.

"It's a Way House in the central valley," Andrew explains. "One of many."

"We've got the situation under control here," Manny answers. And then he grins.

"Operation Angel Pursuit was a success," he says.

"Thank God," Arlene laughs. "Tell Alpha One that we're happy to have him back. I'll pass the news along. The militias will be thrilled."

The ghost of a smile plays across Chris's lips.

Manny explains our situation to Arlene. The color slowly returns to his face, and I realize how incredibly relieved he is that Arlene is alive. It makes me curious...

I share a glance with Chris.

Everything is changing, I think. *The game has shifted again.*

"Get the horses into the stables," Chris commands. "Gather your gear and transfer everything to the vehicles. Armor up, guns up. We're heading home."

Manny continues to talk with Arlene for a while. Chris takes me aside in the house and asks, "What's Manny's relationship with Arlene?"

"He won't tell me." I shrug. "Either he's in love with her or they're just really good friends."

"Huh." Chris plays with the ends of my hair. "Cassie, if Mexico and this Pacific Northwest Alliance are fighting Omega, that means we could actually stand a chance of winning this war."

"I won't believe it until I see it," I say. "But it's a nice thought."

"Ah, ever the eternal optimist."

"I'm being realistic. Omega's got a million soldiers and chemical weapons," I say. "Who's to say that they won't just get a nuclear bomb and kill us all?"

"Because something must be stopping them." He knits his brow. "The threat of retaliation, possibly."

"From who? Us? We practically have no military left."

"I don't know. But I'd like to find out."

I press a kiss against his cheek.

"Let's find out together."

He grins.

When he smiles, I'm reminded of what Vera told me back in Los Angeles – about Chris having been married. I get nauseas just thinking about it. I want to know if the story is true or not. But I am afraid to ask.

Because I'm afraid of what his answer might be.

"Commander," Manny says. He steps inside the house. His hair is as wild as ever. His leather duster is stained with blood and mud and grease. He's a sight to behold – and I realize how much I appreciate this man. This crazy, brilliant pilot from who-knows-where.

"We've got a situation," Manny continues.

My heart sinks.

Another situation?

"What's wrong?" I ask.

"Sector 20 is radio silent," he says. "Either Colonel Rivera never made it back to base or they packed up and moved."

Colonel Rivera. The chief officer of the National Guard unit in Fresno.

I grasp the wall, dizzy.

"You've *got* to be kidding me," I gasp.

"Easy, Cassie," Chris warns, hooking his arm around my waist. "Have you tried contacting other Underground radio outposts? They might know."

"Yes," Manny replies. "Sector 20 just disappeared. If you ask me, that's not a good sign."

Obviously.

"What do we do?" I ask Chris, looking up at his face.

He doesn't answer right away.

Finally he says,

"We go back anyway. And we find what we find."

I hope it's better than what we found here.

Chapter Fifteen

"Light bulb!" I exclaim.

I sit up straight, breaking the monotony of the sound of the engines. I'm sitting in the front seat of an armored Chevrolet Suburban. Chris is driving. Manny and Vera are in another vehicle. Uriah and Derek are in a Humvee, and Andrew is in the backseat, along with a ton of technological supplies and weaponry. We have been driving for two hours, and we have finally broken out of the Tehachapi Mountains. The valley is beautiful this evening, glowing with the orange and pink colors of the sunset.

"What are you talking about?" Chris asks.

"You said Harry was talking about going up north to some kind of a meeting," I say. "Sacramento. That's where he was going."

"You don't think there's some kind of parley going down, do you?" Andrew comments. "Because who the hell would want to parley with Harry Lydell?"

"That makes sense," Chris agrees. "But if Sacramento is a militia stronghold, he shouldn't be anywhere *near* there."

"What if the gathering isn't just a meeting...?" I say. "What if it's a negotiation?"

"That's more likely."

"And if Omega is negotiating, that means they're getting weaker."

"Which means we might be gaining the upper hand."

I hope so. Either that, or Omega is stalling, waiting to make another move.

We don't arrive in Fresno until early morning. It takes hours to rumble through Bakersfield and the surrounding towns in our convoy. As we travel through the darkness, I glimpse flashes of neighborhood subdivisions and shopping centers that have been destroyed in showdowns between militias and Omega. Scout vehicles and motorcycles have been sent ahead to clear the districts for us, but that doesn't put my mind at ease. I close my eyes and try to sleep, anyway.

It doesn't work.

When we arrive in Fresno, I instantly sense something different as we rumble down familiar boulevards like Blackstone and Ashlan. The distant sounds and echoes of gunfire are non-existent. I roll down my window a few inches. Nothing. The dead streetlight at the corner of Herndon and Blackstone has been knocked over. Two buildings have been totally destroyed.

"Something definitely went down while we were gone," Andrew says.

"It wasn't good," I reply.

By the time we reach the entrance to Sector 20, I am expecting the worst. Andrew has been staying in radio contact with the rest of our team in the other vehicles, and their reaction to the current state of Fresno hasn't been good, either.

The chain link fence around the base is broken. I swallow thickly. I haven't seen this place since before we deployed to the Chokepoint to face down Omega's five-million man army. Honestly, I never thought I would see it again.

I figured I'd be dead.

"The base has been compromised," Chris states, stepping on the brakes. A huge chunk of the building is missing – blown apart. We stop the convoy near the front gate. I open the passenger door and walk to the property line. There isn't a soul in sight.

Chris follows me to the gate.

"This was an attack," he says.

"The base is probably still intact inside," I surmise.

"Probably."

"So what do we do?"

"We can't stay here. Rivera is gone."

"Where the hell would he go?" Alexander states, slamming his car door. "Why would he leave?"

Chris takes a moment to answer.

"Our best bet," he replies, "is to keep moving."

"And go where?"

"Sacramento."

"Do you think that's where Rivera went?"

Chris props his boot on the fence.

"There seems to be a correlation, don't you think?" he asks, smiling faintly. "Sacramento is the place to be."

"We don't know what it's like up north," Andrew points out. "It could be totally hostile territory."

"No," Alexander replies. "The Pacific Northwest Alliance – whoever they are - has taken San Francisco, and Mexico is

196

fighting their way from San Diego. I think our chances are better up north than here, actually."

"But who's going to defend the valley?" I say.

"Maybe that's what the gathering in Sacramento will decide," Chris answers. "We need to move now. Every minute we sit here is a minute wasted."

I consider this.

"I agree," I say. "I think we should go, too."

It doesn't come as a surprise to me that no one argues with the decision. With Sector 20 abandoned, what else can we do? It's the only logical option that I can think of.

So we get in our trucks, our SUVs and our Humvees.

And we leave Sector 20 behind.

Again.

The northern part of California is uncharted territory, as far as I'm concerned. Fresno is as far away as I've gotten from Los Angeles since the EMP hit last year. As we drive beyond the city limits, a feeling of anxiety takes hold of me. I realize that without Sector 20, my dad will have no way to find out what happened to me or where I went. Likewise, I'm traveling away from him.

Although I am obviously able to function without my father these days...the fact remains that I am being pulled even farther away from my dad – and the Youngs, and little Isabel. How will Chris's family even know that Jeff died?

They'll probably guess when he never comes home.

But what if *we* never come home, either?

We take the old Highway 99. It runs parallel to the main highway, which is piled high with debris. In some places, the wreckage has been cleared away by Omega troops so they can get their vehicles through. But today everything is silent. There is no troop movement as far as I can see. As we drive closer to residential areas and small towns like Chowchilla and Merced, I see signs of civilization. People on the overpasses, lurking in the shadows. But no military presence.

I don't know if that's a good thing or a bad thing.

"If Sacramento is anything like Los Angeles," I say, "then we're going to have a heck of a time getting inside."

"It's not like Los Angeles," Andrew answers. "It's a rebel stronghold, remember? We should be welcomed with open arms."

"You're forgetting something," I point out. "We *deserted* the National Guard to form this rescue unit, remember? Colonel Rivera isn't exactly going to be pleased to see us."

"What are they going to do?" Chris interjects. "Refuse our help? They need all the help they can get."

"Plus, you *are* Alpha One," I wink.

We hit the city of Ripon. It has taken us four hours - far longer than it would take for a regular traveler. But weaving through backstreets and avoiding potential gang areas takes time. The giant water tower near the edge of the freeway is blackened with smoke. The overpass near the rest area is cracked in two pieces, obstructing the southbound lanes. The drive-in restaurant and gas station looks like they got bombed. There's hardly anything left besides faded signs and piles of rubble.

"Well, isn't this cheery?" Andrew remarks.

"Check in with the others," Chris says.

Andrew snaps his radio on and contacts the other vehicles. So far, so good. Everyone's still here and we haven't run into any trouble. I mean, except for the fact that everything in the state is a freaking garbage dump...yeah. No trouble.

Ripon is only one hour away from Sacramento – driving at freeway speeds. Unfortunately, our travel time is at least double that. As we get closer to the city, the old Highway 99 becomes more difficult to follow, until we have to abandon it altogether. We use maps to navigate through surface streets, getting lost repeatedly in the little towns of Ceres and Lodi.

The scenery here is quite a change from the myriad of dead orchards and hot urban cityscapes of the central valley. Miles of moist marshlands and grazing territory for cattle spread from here to the mountains. The sky is a deep blue. The temperature is cooler.

"I see it!" I exclaim, pointing.

Sacramento is clearly visible in the distance. The skyscrapers gleam against the late evening sunlight. It seems ethereal. A stark contrast to the ravaged skyline of Los Angeles.

"Now that's a nice city," Andrew comments.

"From a distance," Chris replies, untouched.

I study his hands on the wheel. The scars are still there, angry reminders that just over a week ago, he was in a very bad place with very bad people. If anybody has reason to be skeptical, it's Chris.

"So do we just drive in on the freeway or what?" I ask.

"There will be checkpoints leading into the city," Andrew replies. "They'll want us to identify ourselves and our destination. We should be fine. We're militia, not Omega. We're welcome here."

"Welcome is such a relative term," I mutter.

Chris pats my knee. We roll off the side road and hit the freeway. There is no wreckage here. Everything is wide open and clean. The houses along the freeway are abandoned. The bushes and weeds are ridiculously tall.

"This is creepy on so many levels," Andrew says.

We drive beneath a series of overpasses. We are the only vehicles on the road. It *is* creepy, I have to agree. The closer we get to the city, the more tense I become. A city means people and people means trouble.

"Chris," I whisper. "Roadblock."

The freeway is blocked up ahead with two flipped semi-trucks and berms of earth. Military trucks, towers, and personnel as far as the eye can see. A fence around the city limit. Chris and I are in the lead Humvee. Guards in camouflage uniforms monitor our approach. An American flag is flying from the top of the first guard tower.

"Easy, Cassie," Chris says, tapping my cheek with his finger. "They're on *our* side."

The suburban rolls to a stop. Chris turns off the engine. He opens his door. He keeps his hands up – a sign that he means no harm, I guess. A soldier comes out of the guard tower. I open the passenger door and step outside, mimicking Chris's movements, walking toward him. The fence line buzzes with activity. I watch the soldiers. They are eyeing us curiously, but they don't have the expression of men who are alarmed. And I *know* that look.

Chris exchanges a few words with the head guard. I'm on the other side of the car, and his voice is too soft for me to hear above the sound of engines and the wind whipping my hair into circles. In the distance, I hear the sound of a helicopter.

It makes me a bit queasy, given my recent experience.

"And this is...?" I hear the guard say, pointing to me.

"Commander Cassidy Hart," Chris replies. "One of my best."

He flashes a quick, wry grin in my direction. Then he's all business again.

"Well, it's good to see you, Alpha One," the guard finally says. "Tell you the truth, rumor had it that you and your entire militia was dead. If you listen to Rivera tell it, you were dead the day you left."

"Rivera is here?" I say. I walk around the front of the suburban. The rest of the militia remains in their vehicles, waiting for a signal from Chris. A confirmation that we can move forward.

"Yes, ma'am." Closer, the guard is young. Maybe high school – maybe younger. He's barely big enough to carry the rifle in his hands.

Then again, the same goes for me.

"He came through here with his forces, then?" I ask.

"Yes," he replies. "Two weeks ago, ma'am."

"We've heard that there's a rebel meeting going on downtown," Chris tells the guard. "What do you know about that?"

"Well, sir," the boy replies, "they're having a big meeting down at the Capitol Building pretty soon. Rivera, Wright – all the militia commanders and National Guard leaders. Something big is going down. Ever since Mexico and Canada started pushing against the invasion, things have been getting more organized."

Canada, eh?

"How do we get to the Capitol?" I press.

"Follow this road," he says, "and take the third exit."

He continues to give us the rest of the directions.

"You'll have to go through several checkpoints, sir," he tells Chris. "We'll notify the outposts via radio that they should expect you. I can tell you that there's going to be a lot of people that will be happy to hear that you're still alive." He grins at me. "And you too, ma'am."

I feel my cheeks warm and turn toward the city. One skyscraper in particular reflects the sunlight beautifully. The entire building is made of glass that acts as a mirror – almost completely disappearing into the sky. The gates around the roadblock are pulled back. The guard salutes me and walks back to the guardhouse.

"Cassidy..." Chris says, raising an eyebrow. He's standing next to the hood of the car. "Are you ready to do this?"

I meet his strong, steady gaze.

"Yeah," I say. "I'm ready."

And for the first time in a long time, I feel as confident as the words that come out of my mouth.

Chapter Sixteen

I feel like I'm staring down a long, lonely walk at high noon. We're waiting inside the suburban on the other side of a yellow bridge. We have already been through checkpoint after checkpoint. A roiling, muddy river sweeps under the bridge. It has broken the banks at some points, flooding sidewalks and pathways paralleling the river.

Across the bridge, there is a ragged collection of damaged skyscrapers and boulevards, abandoned metropolitan electric rail tracks and empty riverside restaurants. It's the sad remains of civilization. A sick joke. There is nothing here but a military presence and the desperate hope for the return of a civilized society.

We slowly begin moving across the bridge, having already checked in with security at the guardhouse. American flags seem to be everywhere, fluttering from windows, trees and lampposts. People are trying to keep their morale up. They're reminding themselves that this is still America.

I mean, I think it is.

Time will tell.

No one has spoken since we began crossing the bridge. The radio – constantly filled with chatter and code words and updates – is now silent. Maybe I'm not the only one who feels the solemnity of what we're doing. Somewhere deep inside me, I can sense it:

This is going to be a whole new ballgame.

When we roll onto the pavement of the long avenue of Sacramento's Capitol Mall, the Capitol Building and its glittering dome is gleaming white and pure against the dusky evening sky. Somehow it has escaped the effects of the war's devastation. It's lit up like a Christmas tree, glowing with interior lighting. There are blockades and concrete barricades in security rings around the building itself. Soldiers are patrolling and snipers are on top of every building on the strip.

"You think we did the right thing, coming here...?" Andrew whispers.

"Yes," Chris answers. Firm.

There is no hesitation in his answer, and I draw strength from that. As we reach the end of the street, we stop at another checkpoint. The guard there asks for our names and identification. They have been expecting us, and we are directed to take our vehicles to a large building on the north side of the park. We roll into the loading area and get out of our vehicles.

"This is a hotel," I state, looking up at the pretty edifice – there are too many stories for me to count.

"It *was*," Chris corrects. "Now it's a fortress."

And he's right, of course. There are soldiers everywhere. The lobby is huge inside, with shiny flooring and a concierge desk that is being manned by a woman in a National Guard uniform. The sound of phones ringing and the electric lighting inside the building are jarring. It's as if we have stepped into the past – back when things like this were normal. Our team is assigned rooms on the upper floors. Vera looks pleased with the arrangement. I stare at the paper hotel room map that the man at the front desk gives us. He is dressed in uniform, like we are.

"I'm Commander Chris Young," Chris offers. "And this is Commander Hart and our team. We're here for a meeting at the Capitol Building...?"

He leaves the sentence as an open question.

"Yes," the man replies. "It's an honor, sir." He smiles at me. "The negotiations will be held tomorrow morning at oh-eight-hundred. You'll want to find the Senate Chambers – that's where the other militia leaders will be."

"Thank you," Chris says, nodding. "We'll be there."

Andrew, Uriah, Alexander and Manny are studying their hotel maps. They, like me, are scanning for exits and entrances. What is the fastest escape route? Funny how our minds are always on the defensive.

"The elevators are to your left," the man says, pointing.

Chris and I glance at each other.

"Elevators?" I echo.

I follow his line of sight and stare at a row of several elevators. Vera pushes the call button and it lights up. We gaze at it like fascinated children. Andrew is the first one to make a smart remark.

"Look at us," he says, "staring at the pretty lights. You'd think we'd never seen any before."

"Not like this," I reply.

"It's been a while," Uriah agrees.

The elevator arrives. By the time our entire team makes it to the fifteenth floor, we are so in awe of the clean, beautiful surroundings that we are moving in total silence. Maybe it's just the exhaustion of the mission taking its toll. Or maybe we're just really suffering from *that* much culture shock.

I open the door to my room. It's at the end of the hall, across from Chris's. Inside, there is carpet, a bed, and a window that overlooks the street and Capitol Park below. As the rest of the team checks out their new temporary living quarters, I close my eyes and heave a great sigh.

We are safe.

For the time being.

––––––––––––––––––

I sit on the edge of the hotel bed and look around. The room is airtight. Clean, white walls, blue carpet and a gray bedspread. It smells fresh. I stare at my feet, comfortable and laced into brand new combat boots. Dressed head to toe in black – pants, shirt, jacket – I am the epitome of what a sniper should look like. Minus the red hair, of course. *That* is pulled back in a tight military style bun.

I take a deep breath.

It's quiet. No birds, no wind, no gunfire, no shouting. Nothing. I am alone, and I don't like it. I stand up and walk to the window. Six stories up, I have a perfect vantage point of the street. I could easily kill anyone before they even had a chance to reach the front of the building.

And it frightens me a little – that I think of things like this. That the first thing I see when I look out a window is a tactical opportunity.

"Cassie?"

Someone knocks on the hotel door. I turn my back on the window and look through the peephole, even though I know who it is. Chris. I open the door. He's standing there, wearing a black outfit, same as me. He has cleaned up well. He looks professional and handsome. Every bit the model commander.

"Are you ready?" he asks, raising an eyebrow.

"Sure," I reply. A little bit too fast.

"Maybe I should ask again."

"Don't. I'm fine." I take a step backward as he moves into the room, closing the door behind him. "This is no big deal. It's not like we're walking into a firefight, right?"

"No," Chris says. "This is a different kind of fight."

I lean against the wall, exhausted and afraid.

"What good is this going to do?" I whisper. "Sitting around and talking about everything is just going to make people mad at each other. Remember when we talked about rebuilding the government at Camp Freedom? My dad was about ready to throw punches over the difference in opinion."

"At some point, it has to be discussed," Chris shrugs. "I'd rather do it now than later. If we wait, we may not have the chance."

"I guess." I sigh. "You handle the talking, okay? I'll mess it up."

"Don't be naïve, Cassie," Chris replies. "You won't mess anything up." He places one hand on each side of me on the wall. "You can do anything. You're strong."

I press my lips together.

"It's different," I insist.

"No. It's not." Chris kisses my forehead. "Just relax."

"Right. Because it's so easy to relax."

He smiles a little.

"No. Because it's healthy," he says.

He presses his lips against mine. I slip my hands behind his neck and melt into him, his strong hands gripping my back. He tastes like coffee. I pull back for a moment.

"We're in this together," I say. "We're a team."

"Yeah. Of course." He gives me a puzzled look. "And we act like one."

I nod. And I kiss him again, heady with his scent and his touch. There is no place in the world I would rather be – regardless of the apocalypse. A few moments later, Chris holds me at arm's length.

"I'm proud of you," he states. "No matter what happens."

"Ditto," I grin.

I take one last look around the hotel room before we walk out the door. There are no sounds as we take the elevator to the bottom floor. The lobby area is heavily guarded with troops. I ache to hold Chris's hand as we walk here, but it wouldn't be professional. Outside, there are vehicles and guardhouses. Armed soldiers. Checkpoints and more checkpoints. It feels good to be on the inside of this steel ring of protection – rather than the other way around.

I almost feel safe.

Almost.

We cross the street. Capitol Park is beautiful. The grass is green again and the hedges have been trimmed. The American rebels have wasted no time in cleaning up the place. The sparkling white exterior of the Capitol building itself is stunning, reminiscent of a Greek temple or an amphitheater – white pillars and marble statues. The bronze Great Seal of the State of California is preserved in concrete in front of the building.

A long canvas tent is pushed up against the entrance. Chris and I walk inside. There are enough guards to form a small rescue unit inside. We go through the checkpoint and enter the building.

In wartime, we are allowed to keep our firearms.

It's one of those necessary things.

"Which way?" I whisper.

We stand at the mouth of a long hallway. White flooring. Glass cases are set up against the wall. Each case displays miniature scenes of different counties in California. Cities, agricultural communities, beachside resorts. How it used to be.

"Can I help you find something?"

A guard approaches us. He's young and handsome.

"We're looking for the Senate Chambers," Chris states. "We're here for the negotiations."

"You're Commander Young," the guard states, staring. "And you're Commander Hart."

Chris nods slightly.

"An honor, sir," the guard says. "Um, yes, sir. The Senate Chambers are up these stairs here and on the third floor. You'll see the people."

"Thank you, soldier," Chris replies.

We climb the stairs and enter a hallway full of echoes. I lean in closer to Chris and whisper, "How do people know who we are?"

Chris gives me an amused look as we follow the curve of the hallway. I tilt my head up and marvel at the inside of the capitol dome. The sunlight is shining through the windows, illuminating the colorful design. A massive marble statue of Queen Isabella of Spain and Christopher Columbus sits in the center of the rotunda, surrounded by velvet ropes.

"Fancy," I comment.

"The Capitol *was* a museum, too, before the EMP," Chris tells me.

"And you know this because...?"

"Because I came here before the war. To meet the governor."

"Why?"

We find the staircase. It wraps around both sides of the rotunda, lined with red carpet.

"Chris?" I press. "Why did you meet the governor?"

"I was...honored for my service overseas before I was discharged," he says.

"You must have been some soldier." I smile. "I'm not surprised."

Chris doesn't look happy about it.

We climb to the third level. There are people here. Many of them are dressed in business suits – but most are dressed in whatever clothes they could find. Chris and I are not the only ones here wearing a uniform. There are others. Giant, wooden double doors lead into a seating area that wraps around a room two stories below. The Senate Chambers. The seats are packed. It looks like a Roman courtroom.

"You're in the wrong part of the Capitol, Commander."

I turn at the sound of a familiar voice.

"Angela!" I exclaim.

I throw my arms around her neck in a hug. A hug of complete, utter relief. She's wearing a green uniform, her hair pulled back. She straightens her spine, startled by my expression of emotion.

"Good to see you back, Commander Young," she breathes, smiling. "Thank God you're here."

Um, hello. I'm here, too.

"Thank you," Chris replies, ever the gentleman. "Good to see you, too, Angela."

"You two are militia officers," she says. "You need to be downstairs inside the Senate Chambers, not above it. This area is for civilians."

"Where's Colonel Rivera?" I ask.

No sense beating around the bush.

"He's with the officers, of course," she replies. "Follow me, please."

She turns on her heel and we follow her back down the staircase.

"It's been a while since you've been back here, hasn't it?" Angela asks Chris.

As always, she makes a point of ignoring me. Like mother like daughter, I suppose.

"A few years," Chris replies.

Angela keeps walking. I lower my voice, anxiety curling in the pit of my stomach as we get closer to the Senate Chambers.

"Vera told me that you knew Angela when you were stationed in Coronado," I whisper. "Is that true?"

Chris says nothing. Then,

"Yes, it's true."

"Why didn't you tell me?"

"It didn't seem necessary."

A couple of the guards allow Angela to pass through some heavy double doors. We follow suit and step into a foyer. Green carpet is everywhere, and so are ornate carved pillars and velvet curtains.

"She told me something else," I continue. My hands are trembling. "She told me you were married, Chris." I take a deep breath. "I've been meaning to ask you about it for days...but I couldn't..."

Chris's face remains unmoved. Expressionless. He is the picture of calm. The only hint of an emotional reaction is the muscle that ticks in his jaw.

Angela whirls around suddenly and we stop.

"When you enter this room," she warns, "be on your guard. Everything that you say will be scrutinized. The rebel leaders gathered here want to hear what you think. We must be united." She turns her steely gaze on Chris. "Understood?"

Chris doesn't reply. He doesn't need to.

Of *course* he understands.

She leads us through another pair of doors. The room is wide. It's an open floor, dotted with dozens of desks. The desks are empty – no computers, no name holders. Just paper and notepads. Rebel leaders dressed in a variety of different uniforms are sitting down. It's similar to a courtroom setting. Three seats at the front of the room are on a raised platform. A man with gray hair and a handsome, weathered face is sitting there, dressed in a suit and tie. He watches Chris and I enter. There is a woman that I do not recognize on his left, and on his right...is Colonel Rivera. He's dressed in uniform. When he sees me, his expression freezes.

He is not angry.

He is *furious.*

And when he realizes that Chris is with me, I'm pretty sure a vein starts to bulge in his forehead. I swallow a nervous lump in my throat and absently follow Chris's hushed command to sit. It dawns on me that everyone in the room – above and below – is staring at us.

Cassidy Hart and Chris Young.

Maybe we're more infamous than we think.

I grasp the handles of the wooden chair and stare at the desk. Chris is beside me.

"Breathe," he whispers. "You've got this."

"Shall we call this meeting to order?" The man speaking is sitting in the middle chair on the raised podium. He looks very distinguished.

I look around me. Men, women. Uniforms that I recognize, uniforms that I don't recognize. And most of them are staring at us. I vaguely realize that Vera, Uriah, Manny, Andrew and Alexander are sitting above us in the spectator seats. Uriah nods, never taking his eyes from me.

The distinguished-looking man bangs a heavy gavel on the table in front of him and announces in a deep, baritone voice, "I hereby declare this California State Convention of Leaders open." He pauses and scans the room with a fierce gaze. "My name is Robert Lockwood, and I am the presiding Speaker of the House, Pro Tem. We are gathered in this hall – in this building – to negotiate and formulate a plan of action against the invading forces of Omega."

His voice is incredibly rich and deep. I watch him carefully as he speaks, looking for any signs of insincerity. It's hard to tell.

"I want to extend a welcome to Colonel Rivera of the California National Guard," he continues, "and thank him for his valiant contribution to improving the security of Sacramento."

A short burst of applause echoes throughout the room.

I want to roll my eyes, but I don't.

"And thank you – *all* of you – for making the journey here today," Lockwood says. "You are all well respected leaders in the individual militias throughout the state of California, and your efforts to defeat Omega is appreciated more than I could ever personally express. You are the lifeblood in this war. You are the reason that we can meet here today."

More applause. I study Chris's face.

He is not impressed.

"Our strongest militia forces in California have been concentrated in the Great Central Valley and in the Sierra Nevada Mountains," Lockwood says. "And for that, we have two men to thank. Commander Frank Hart of the Mountain Rangers and Commander Chris Young of the Freedom Fighters and the combined militia forces of the Great Central Valley."

The applause is thunderous this time around. I twist in my seat, shocked. My father is standing near the back of the room, dressed in militiaman garb. He's wearing the customary uniform of the Mountain Rangers – the six-pointed star stitched into his sleeve. We lock eyes and I feel the breath leave my lungs.

"Dad," I whisper.

"Cassidy," he nods, smiling.

There are tears in his eyes. But we don't move. We can't.

Chris smiles meaningfully at me. I barely manage to turn my attention back to Lockwood as he begins speaking again.

My heart is racing in my chest. I feel faint, dizzy. I've been worried about my dad ever since I left Camp Freedom two months ago.

Thank you, God. Thank you.

Who else is here, I wonder?

"We might as well tackle the issue at hand," Lockwood says, placing his hands on the railing in front of him. "The Pacific Northwest Alliance – specifically, Oregon - is moving in from the north and Mexico is pushing from the south. Omega is relentless in their naval and land attacks on the western coastline, but the Alliance has managed to push them out of San Francisco, and most of Oregon."

Angela raises her hand.

"The Senate recognizes Commander Wright," Lockwood says.

"What about Mexico?" she asks. "Where are they headed?"

"They have secured San Diego," Lockwood replies. "The east coast is engaged in pitched combat. The United States military has amassed what forces they have left and concentrated on Florida, New York and Texas. Omega is sending an army from the east, and they will attempt to send millions more through the central valley."

"We stopped their advance from the south," Colonel Rivera bellows. "We can do it again."

"We'll need more than simple strategy this time around," Angela says, leveling her gaze at the Colonel. She's seated at a desk, legs crossed. Cool as a cucumber. "We are surrounded on all sides by millions of soldiers. We need manpower *and* firepower."

"Which brings us to the ultimate question," Lockwood replies.

The tension crackles in the room as Colonel Rivera glares daggers at Angela.

"Canada and Mexico have proposed an alliance with the state of California," Lockwood announces. "Since the dissolution of the Federal Government, and until such a time as the reformation of the United States of America, each state stands alone. We make our decisions on our own. Oregon and Washington have already allied themselves with what is being called the Pacific Northwest Alliance. If we combine our forces with theirs, our chances of succeeding in stopping Omega's advance into the United States – or at least the west coast – are significantly higher."

Chris and I look at each other.

So this is what the big news is.

"An alliance is not something to be taken lightly," I hear my father volunteer.

"Allying with another country – or in this case, *two* countries – changes the dynamics of our war," Chris adds. His voice is strong and clear. I can't help it: my heart swells with pride hearing him talk. "But in my opinion we can use all the help we can get. Face it, we're fighting for our lives. Omega kicked in the front *and* back door, and right now is the moment of truth. We fight or we die. It's as simple as that."

"And what if Canada and Mexico end up turning their backs on us?" a woman in a Navy uniform asks. "What if we succeed in pushing Omega out and they decide to stay here?"

"What if Omega succeeds in invading our country and *they* stay here?" I say, standing up suddenly. My voice wavers for a moment. "Here's the truth: Omega is going to destroy us. Period. We are doomed if we don't get help. Grassroots militia groups and the remains of a National Guard force will only do so much. We need *more* than that.

"The survival of the only free nation left on the planet is at stake. Our lives are at stake. We have to get united on this. Right now, the only reason that we're able to meet in Sacramento is because of what Canada and Mexico has done in the north and in the south. Without them, Omega would have held San Francisco and San Diego and we'd be pushed out of here, too."

"How do we know we can trust the alliance?" Colonel Rivera growls.

"You're a fool if you think that we can win this on our own," I reply. The room falls silent. "We need help. Desperately." I step into the aisle, overcome with a powerful urge to say what needs to be said. "Look, I've been in this fight since day one. I have seen what Omega has done, just like everyone else in this room. I saw what they did to the city I grew up in. And I've seen what they've done to my friends and family." I take a breath and steady my voice. "I've held my friends in my arms as they've bled to death on the battlefield," I say, softer. "I've seen children digging through garbage in the gutter just to stay alive." I open my arms up. "And you think there's some kind of question about whether or not we should accept help? We are *dying*, my friends. This is it. We won't get a second chance. So make the right choice. For God. For country. Whatever it is you believe in. Please. An alliance will help us. Choose the destruction of Omega, because that holds the promise of freedom. This is the right thing to do."

I clench my fists, the rush of determination making my speech bolder.

"I think it was Ben Franklin who said that if the revolutionary war heroes didn't hang together, they would all hang separately," I continue. "I'm not a great historian, but let's look at the facts. If we *don't* stand united, Omega will take us down. But together, we stand a chance. *I* choose freedom. *I* choose to fight, even if it means I might die. Because I won't live like this, in Omega's shadow. There's too much at stake. Stand together. Right now, unity is our most powerful weapon. Let's utilize it. We can do it." I look at Lockwood. "We just have to make the right choice *now*."

Thick tension settles over the room. I turn around and look at Chris. He is staring at me, and then he tips his head in a slight nod. In the back, somebody starts clapping. It's probably my dad. He *would*. It's followed by more applause, and then the audience above our heads is standing up, and so are the rebel leaders in the room.

And I realize that they are clapping for me.

For all of us.

It seems to go on forever, until the applause is broken by the Speaker of the House.

"Well said, Commander Hart," Lockwood speaks. "Unite or die. Freedom or enslavement. It is a harsh truth, but a truth nevertheless."

"Hart is right," Angela says. "We must stand united."

"I agree," a man in a Marine uniform says. "Liberty or death. The options are clear, and we have to make the choice to form a united front."

There is a tumultuous bout of cheering and agreement from the civilians in the seats above. The officers in the Senate Chambers are lifting their fists into the air, shouting things like, "Liberty or death!" and "Hart is right, we need to join the Alliance!"

"The majority vote rules," Lockwood says. "California will join the Alliance, and together, we will combine with the states of the west coast, as well as the countries of Mexico and Canada, in our stand against Omega's invasion."

More cheering. More raised fists. More backslapping. I have not moved from my standing position, and a feeling of sweet relief sweeps over me.

This is the right thing to do. I can feel it.

"California must have representation to the Alliance," Lockwood continues. "As such, I propose that we appoint a senator to represent California's interests in the negotiations with representatives from the Pacific Northwest Alliance: Washington, Oregon, Canada and Mexico."

"We need someone who understands what we have been through," Dad interjects. "Somebody who knows what's at stake."

"Where will these negotiations take place?" someone asks.

"That has yet to be determined," Lockwood replies.

"Will we be negotiating between the states and countries – or will we also be negotiating with Omega?" Angela asks.

"Both," Lockwood says. He is silent for a moment. And for some reason, I know what is going to happen before it does.

"Any nominations?" he asks.

"I nominate Cassidy Hart." Angela stands at her desk. She does not look at me.

"I second that nomination," Dad says.

Oh, God. No. Not me. Please.

Why did I have to open my mouth and talk?

"I support the nomination as well," Chris says. He stands.

The room is a chorus of agreement. The majority of the rebel leaders – Colonel Rivera excluded – are on their feet, and the audience is in an excited frenzy. I feel ill. Overwhelmed.

Why me...?

People all around me are talking. There is noise, activity. The militia leaders and military officers are speaking to each other, and many of them are...smiling. They are happy. I look at Chris. He squeezes my shoulder. I can see pride in his eyes.

"The decision is unanimous, Commander Hart," Lockwood booms. His voice is a blur in the background. "You have been nominated for the position of Interim State Senator to represent California in the Pacific Northwest Alliance."

I am dazed. I stare at him, nodding vaguely. I feel myself move my head, and I know the instant that I do that I am committed on an entirely new level. This is bigger. This is different. This is new.

I scarcely believe it when I say, "I accept."

Because the words have to be spoken.

"Thank you, Commander Hart," he says. "Ladies and gentleman, I present to you: Senator Cassidy Hart of the Great State of California."

More applause. I am burning up, flushed with energy and excitement and the realization that this is a *good* thing. We are building a stable, structured system with which to fight Omega. We are allying ourselves with strong countries and friends. We are pooling our resources. We are standing united.

Hope blossoms in my chest.

This truly *is* new.

Militia leaders that I have never seen before flood to my desk, shaking Chris's hand and mine. Angela embraces me for the first time in...well, ever. My father walks through the crowd and I throw my arms around his neck.

"We made it," I say.

"Yes," he replies. "We did." He smiles. "Senator."

I shake my head. Chris gives me a gentle hug. He whispers softly,

"You did the right thing."

I look at his face.

"I know," I reply.

And it is not a lie.

The commotion inside the Senate Chambers exudes a positive, vibrant energy. These people are filled with hope. It is infectious, and it is the first time since the EMP hit Los Angeles that I have felt this much encouragement. It is a miracle. I find myself closing my eyes and saying a silent prayer of thanks.

We have come so far...and although we still have a long way to go, we have accomplished much. Chris and I leave the Senate Chambers, Dad and Angela following us. Colonel Rivera has been lost somewhere in the crowd, and that is fine with me. I am no longer afraid of his wrath. I did what needed to be done, and it was the right thing.

Vera, Alexander, Uriah, Andrew and Manny are waiting for us in the hallway.

"You're crazy," Vera states.

That is all she says, but there is a slight smile on her face. Slight. Uriah is grinning like a proud older brother, and Alexander seems almost at ease.

"Not bad, Cassidy," Andrew comments.

"Well, Senator," Manny exclaims. "The world awaits you."

"So dramatic," I laugh. "Thank you, Manny."

"For...?"

"For everything."

I am overcome with the solemnity of the fact that everyone around me – at some point or another – has played a part in all of us getting this far. Especially Manny.

"Shall we adjourn to the great outdoors?" Manny suggests, winking. "It's a little stuffy in here. All these politicians."

Chris chuckles.

"They're hardly politicians," he says.

"Let's just get outside," I agree.

We follow the hallways, descend the staircase and leave the Capitol Building. It is a beautiful day, and from where we stand on the front steps, we have a perfect view of the entire boulevard, ending with the yellow bridge that crosses the Sacramento River.

"Everything's different now," I say. Just loud enough for Chris to hear me. "It's all going to change."

"Change is a good thing," Chris replies, touching my cheek.

We walk to the edge of the park, cross the street, and stop at a water fountain surrounded with rose bushes. One library building sits on each side of the fountain, graced with Greek marble statues.

I meet Chris's gaze, and I feel the camaraderie of the people around me – Vera included. I wrap my fingers around Chris's hand and look back at the Capitol. Maybe it represents more than just a meeting place. Maybe it represents the starting point of a new era. Of something better. Of recovery and strength and rebuilding.

"Let's go home," I say.

As the words pass my lips, a deep, jarring rumble breaks the silence of the quiet Capitol grounds. It is a sound and a feeling that I am all too familiar with. The windows near the corner of the Capitol Building shatter, sending shards of glass through the air. I am knocked off my feet. I hit the ground on my knees. Chris grabs my arm and we crouch on the cement, behind the fountain and the roses. Billows of ash and dust rise from the base of the stately structure. There is screaming in the distance. Somewhere, a siren wails.

I stare in abject horror. The soldiers roll in and the security units engage.

And I watch as the dome of the Capitol Building collapses in a cloud of smoke and fire.

Epilogue

Tick, tock.

Time. Not so long ago, it was important to me. I lived my life on a clock. Time to get up. Time for breakfast. Time for work. Time for lunch.

It was always precious. Never enough minutes in the day.

It's odd to me, then, how little time means anymore. The days blur together and the hours of the clock become one. I have no appointments to keep, no friends to meet with. My life is a never-ending cycle of grinding, gritty, warfare. The days become weeks and the weeks become months. There is no pause in the brutality that is found here.

I am twenty years old. The girl who left Los Angeles afraid and unsure after an EMP last year no longer exists. She has been remade.

The girl is gone. The soldier remains.

I have lost everything. My home, my friends, my country. But I have gained so much, too. My father, Chris, my fellow soldiers and the men and women that fearlessly went into the heart of Los Angeles to rescue their commander. There might be destruction, but I have found great loyalty. There might be death, but I have found life. There might be hatred, but I have found love. There is still hope. There is still a chance. For those of us who are willing to fight back, the situation is not as bleak as it seems.

The war has only just begun.

And I'm ready for it.

To Be Continued in

State of Alliance

Book 5 the Collapse Series

More Titles from Summer Lane:

About the Author

Summer Lane is the #1 bestselling author of the *Collapse Series, Zero Trilogy, Bravo Saga, Collapse: The Illustrated Guide* and the adventure thriller, *Unbreakable SEAL.*

Summer owns WB Publishing. She is an accomplished journalist and creative writing teacher. She also owns an online magazine, Writing Belle, where she has interviewed and worked with countless authors from around the globe.

Summer lives in the Central Valley of California with her husband, where she enjoys reading, collecting tea, visiting the beach and the mountains, and counting down the days until she has her very own puppy (if you've read *Bravo: Apocalypse Mission,* you'll understand).

Connect with Summer online at:

Summerlaneauthor.com

WritingBelle.com

Twitter: @SummerEllenLane

Facebook: @SummerLaneAuthor

Email Summer with thoughts or comments at:

summerlane101@gmail.com

Acknowledgements

Writing a series is somewhat like an endless state of pursuit – a constant race to create a story that will do the characters justice and open audience's imaginations to new adventures and dramas. This book was one of the most detailed novels I have ever written. From combat uniforms to tactical strategies, *State of Pursuit* would not exist without the technical expertise and experience of Don Lane. Cassidy Hart and Chris Young have survived the apocalypse because of him. Thank you, thank you, thank you! I am also immeasurably grateful for the editing work by Dave Hudiburgh, a seasoned veteran himself and a wonderful friend. I want to thank my mother and my brother for being incredibly supportive of the work that I do, in addition to my grandparents, Pete and Nancy. You are all wonderful and I love you very much!

The online community of bloggers and book reviewers has been unendingly supportive of The Collapse Series, and you have my eternal gratitude! Thank you to my many writer friends – you know who you are! – who have been there for me during this crazy, wonderful journey. Thank you James and Janice White. I would not be a writer at all if it weren't for you two. I love you both. Thank you Ellen Mansoor Collier, for being an ardent supporter of my writing endeavors, and for being my friend.

To my friends and my family that has been so warm and welcoming to a girl that writes stories for a living – thank you. Your kindness will never be forgotten. In just a little over one year's time, I have been able to publish four bestselling novels, start a publishing company, develop a creative writing curriculum program and begin work on many other exciting and wonderful projects. That in itself is a testament to the grace and goodness of God's blessing. Without Him I would not have the gift of writing, and Cassidy Hart and Chris Young would have never existed. I am always and forever grateful for this. God is good.

Romans 8:28

CPSIA information can be obtained
at www.ICGtesting.com
Printed in the USA
LVOW01s2254130317

527109LV00008B/145/P